DEATH IN THE AIR

BOOK 10 IN THE DI GILES SERIES

ANNA-MARIE MORGAN

ALSO BY ANNA-MARIE MORGAN

In the DI Giles Series:

Book 1 - Death Master

Book 2 - You Will Die

Book 3 - Total Wipeout

Book 4 - Deep Cut

Book 5 - The Pusher

Book 6 - Gone

Book 7 - Bone Dancer

Book 8 - Blood Lost

Book 9 - Angel of Death

DEATH IN THE AIR

Copyright © 2019 by Anna-marie Morgan
All rights reserved.

No part of this book may be reproduced in any form or by any electronic or mechanical means, including information storage and retrieval systems, without written permission from the author, except for the use of brief quotations in a book review.

For my mum, with love.

1

OUT OF THE BLUE

A sickening thunderclap echoed across the sky, reverberating against the buildings and aircraft hangars at Welshpool Airport.

Witnesses below held their hands up, shielding their eyes from the sun, mouths hanging slack-jawed as they watched the pieces of wreckage slam to the ground.

The explosion threw up thick plumes of black smoke, billowing above russet flames, reaching skyward.

Panicked cries went out from the observers, who broke their frozen silence to run towards the carnage, desperate to find survivors. Several cried when they realised their efforts were futile.

∽

THE STENCH of burning engine oil stung her nostrils and burned the back of her throat. Yvonne's blouse stuck to her back, in what threatened to be a record temperature for the end of September. It wasn't the heat knotting her stomach, but the unbidden images of her husband's plane crash ten years earlier.

She shook her head to clear it.

"Head-on, ma'am." Callum wiped his forehead with the back of his hand.

"But how?" Yvonne frowned, raising her own hand to shield her eyes as she peered skyward. "Look up there. Just look. Not even a suggestion of cloud. There's no wind. There's barely a breeze. How the hell did two planes collide in these conditions?"

Callum shrugged. "That would be why we're here, ma'am."

The DI frowned. "Well, obviously." She sighed. "Let's see what's inside the cordon."

As ambulances transported the last of the bodies from the scene, Yvonne took in the mangled mess that had been two planes. They couldn't see it all. The wreckage had fallen over a considerable area. But she could see enough. Enough of the smashed metal, the burned interiors, the faces on those who had witnessed the horror first-hand.

She felt a familiar fear well within her, her own memories so vivid, even now. She turned her face away to wipe the tears.

2

A COMPELLING WITNESS

Two days later, and Yvonne was back at the airport to interview a witness who claimed he had seen everything.

As she locked her car in the airport carpark, Ryan Aston approached her with a languid stride, his cat-like figure, amplified by his height. Beyond them, the enormous hangar that comprised the bulk of the airport building.

He ran his eyes over her face as though to read her thoughts.

Yvonne estimated him to be around thirty-five. His hair, auburn and short. Military style.

"Inspector Giles?" He held out his hand, his eyes, unblinking.

"Yes, that's me. How do you do? I take it you are Ryan Aston?" She took the offered hand, wondering why her words had sounded so formal.

He nodded. "I am, for my sins." He smiled, but his gaze unnerved her.

"I understand you witnessed the collision, and what led up to it?"

"I did."

Yvonne looked about them. The accident site remained cordoned off, the blue and white tape flapping in the breeze. She took out her notebook, leaning it on the gatepost. "Is here all right?"

The heavens opened. He cast his gaze skyward, then flicked his head towards a black Audi to his left. "That's my car. We can sit inside. It's a little bigger than..." He eyed her Renault.

Yvonne's facial muscles twitched, but she controlled the temptation to insist they use hers. "Sure, why not?" She clicked her notebook closed. "After you."

"What do you do for a living, Mr Aston?" she asked, once seated. She could not help eyeing with envy the interior of the vehicle and the light reflecting off the various dust-free surfaces. Her nostrils flared at the pungent smell of polish.

"I'm an engineer. I design parts at a machine plant on the other side of Welshpool."

"Why were you at the airport on the day of the accident?"

He stared through the windscreen, giving her his profile view. "I have a friend who is a pilot. Light aircraft, mostly. I'd come down hoping to speak to him."

"What is your friend's name?"

"Tim. Tim Payne."

"And, did you see him?"

He shook his head. "I'd missed him by about twenty minutes. I was heading back to my car when I saw a one-engine plane, a Piper, overhead. It was behaving erratically."

"In what way?" Yvonne tilted her head to hear him as the rain battered the roof of the car.

"It was yawing as though the pilot was fighting with the controls, or there was a problem on board."

"Could you see any smoke? Fire?"

"No. Nothing like that."

"Did the engine sound strange?"

"As far as I could tell, the engine sounded fine. And I would have noticed if it didn't. I've been around light aircraft for most of my life. I'm not a pilot myself, but I enjoy going up with friends who are."

"And one of these would be Tim Payne?"

"Yes. I've been up with Tim many times."

"You say you'd just missed him. Where was he?"

"He'd flown out. Shropshire way."

"Is this controlled airspace?"

He shook his head. "No. They use visual cues to avoid accidents. They ground flights in bad weather."

"So, tell me more about what happened and what you saw."

"The first plane circled at least twice. Big circles, yawing from side-to-side. I kept watching, hoping the pilot would sort out whatever the problem was, but then I saw the second plane coming in. Again, this was a single-engine craft, a Cessna. It was making an approach to land, and he gave the first plane a wide berth, by flying at a lower level."

"Okay."

"Then the first plane did the oddest thing." He pressed his lips together, shaking his head.

"Go on."

"It seemed to make a beeline for the second craft which attempted evasive action by banking into a turn, but the Piper adjusted to it and looked to speed up, right before the collision. There was a massive bang and bits of aircraft began raining down."

Yvonne had given up taking notes and, instead, recorded what Aston said on her mobile. "And you're sure that the first aircraft looked like it was deliberately seeking the other plane?"

"I'm sure it was."

"Could it be that it was having problems flying a straight course and that it inadvertently crossed into the other airplane's path? You said it had been yawing."

"I know I did, but it appeared to make a turn for the other plane and dive. It's possible that mechanical problems accounted for it, but it looked deliberate to me. The plane adjusted its course more than once to hit that other plane."

Yvonne stared at him, lips pursed. "Hmm."

Her eyes wandered over the immaculate dash and grit-free carpeting. "Is this freshly valeted?"

He sat back in his seat, mouth partially open, a frown creasing his forehead. "Well, yes, actually. Why?"

She shrugged. "No reason. It just looks it, that's all."

"I get it done regularly. At least, once a month."

"Where do you go? Mine could do with a clean."

"I use the little place on the Lion Works estate, near Newtown."

She nodded. "I know the one, thanks."

"Am I free to go now?" He placed his hands on the steering wheel.

"Sure. What's the best way to reach you?"

He gave her his mobile number.

"Thank you." As she left his car, she rubbed her chin, her eyes glazed in thought.

3

UNCOMFORTABLE BEDFELLOWS

The nostril-teasing smell of garlic, herbs and wine enveloped her like a well-worn jumper as she entered the front door. Tasha was home.

She tossed her keys and bag down on the hall table and wandered through to the kitchen, placing a light kiss on the psychologist's cheek, as the latter laid the place settings on the island. "Hey, good-looking-"

"It's a beef casserole." Tasha laughed. "And I may have overdone the garlic."

Yvonne grinned. "You can never have too much garlic."

"A whole bulb?"

"Okay, maybe you can overdo the garlic. I'll try not to breathe on anyone at work tomorrow." She took a bottle of red from the wooden rack on the kitchen counter, and two glasses from the cupboard, elbowing it shut.

"Good day?" Tasha asked, concentrating on the removal of the casserole from the oven, pulling her head back as a steam cloud billowed up.

"Busy." Yvonne sighed. "And draining. I'm glad to be home."

Tasha smiled. "I hope you're hungry, too."

"I'm ravenous." The DI poured a generous glass each and, as they ate, the psychologist gazed at her, the skin around her eyes, creasing.

"Are you all right?" Yvonne asked, eventually.

"There's something I need to tell you." Tasha caught her bottom lip between her teeth.

"Uh oh." The DI paused between mouthfuls.

"I've got to go away for a week or two. The Met have asked me to help them with a case of national importance."

"Wow." Yvonne scratched her head. "That's sounds intriguing."

"Yes, and they haven't explained what the case is, yet, but they want my help as soon as I can be there."

"When are you leaving?" Yvonne's heart sank. She was getting used to having Tasha with her in the evenings. She didn't relish the thought of being without her.

"Tomorrow morning, I'm afraid." Tasha sighed. "I'll miss you, DI Giles." She tilted her head, double-blinking at her companion.

"I'll miss you, too." The DI gave her a wistful smile. "I miss you already."

"I wish I didn't have to go, but we need the income."

"You know, we could have work coming up here for you in Dyfed-Powys."

"Well, that sounds good, but I'm not sure your superiors would look favourably on my working with you, now that we are partners."

Yvonne stared at her hands.

"You have told them, haven't you?"

The DI pulled at her lips, her eyes narrowing. She grimaced.

"You haven't told them."

"Not exactly. Not in so many words..." She shook her head and sighed. "I haven't told them."

Tasha's face dropped. "Oh."

"I intend to. I just haven't found the right moment."

"The right moment?" The psychologist frowned. "You're embarrassed to admit it to them?"

"No. Yes. I don't know. Sometimes, I'm not so brave." Yvonne's eyes dropped to the countertop.

"It's okay." Tasha reached across the table to cup the DI's hand with her own. "I'll leave you to judge when the time is right. Besides, it leaves the door open for me to work with the team again. What they don't know, they can't object to."

Yvonne smiled and nodded, but inside, her gut knotted with guilt.

∿

Dewi poured their coffees as Yvonne chewed the tip of her pen, still dwelling on her conversation with Tasha.

"Worried about something, ma'am?" He handed her a mug.

She shook her head. "I'm fine. We have the meeting with Llewelyn in five. You ready?"

"As I'll ever be." Dewi eyed the paperwork on his desk, his face tense. "Think it'll take long?"

She shrugged. "I've no idea. Never can tell with Chris. It'll depend on what it's about. If it's about the case, based on what we have so far? It'll be over in two minutes."

Dewi pulled a face. "It's only been a few days. He won't expect too much."

The DI listened at the door before giving it two raps.

"Come in."

He didn't sound irritated. She straightened her skirt and took a deep breath.

"Ah, Yvonne and Dewi, come in. Take a seat." Llewelyn ran a hand through his hair as he pointed them to chairs alongside his desk, where a bespectacled man in his fifties sorted through papers in a file.

"This is Dr. Gethin Jenkins." Llewelyn nodded to the man. "He is a Human Factors Inspector with the Air Accidents Investigation Branch. They asked him in to examine our Welshpool collision, because the accident resulted in deaths of the pilots and a passenger."

The two detectives shook hands with Jenkins, the DI determined not to stare at the pronounced comb-over in his ash-grey hair. "DI Yvonne Giles, and this is my sergeant, DS Dewi Hughes. Pleased to meet you," she said as she took a seat at right angles to him.

Llewelyn handed a mug to Jenkins, before joining them. "They have tasked Dr. Jenkins with looking into the professional and personal lives of the pilots and passenger of the aircraft involved in the Welshpool incident. I've explained that your team, Yvonne, have already gathered a good deal of information, and that you will share this with him. The need for our teams to work together is clear, and you may wish to accompany Gethin on his field investigation."

The DI nodded. "That would be good. We've had some interesting accounts from witnesses." She pursed her lips. "One of whom firmly believes he saw the Piper aircraft flying erratically before appearing to collide on purpose with the other. He agreed that mechanical problems might account for what he saw, but still felt it was a deliberate act."

Gethin Jenkins cleared his throat. "It's a precarious thing, relying on witness interpretation, as I'm sure you are aware, but that is the sort of information I need to form a fuller picture of the events."

Yvonne nodded. "Of course."

"Gethin has three weeks with us, initially, to gather as much information as possible-"

"Three weeks?" The DI frowned. "That's not very long."

"Oh, I'll likely be spending months delving into the backgrounds of the men, but I don't have to complete everything in the field. Plus, there'll be other guys popping over to do their bit, engineering inspectors etc, dealing with the mechanical workings of the planes. My information runs alongside theirs. They called me in because the collision resulted in several deaths and I'm a local."

"So, you are from around here?" Dewi took a sip from his mug.

Jenkins nodded. "Brecon."

"We've had a few fatal accidents in Powys over the last six months." Yvonne's eyes glazed over as though she was seeing them in her mind.

"We have noticed." Jenkins put his coffee mug down on the carpet. "However, clusters can happen, statistically, and we shouldn't read too much into it without evidence of a link."

Yvonne narrowed her eyes at him.

He puffed his chest out. "We receive between five- and seven hundred accident reports a year at the AAIB. We send inspectors out to thirty or forty of them, usually just the fatal ones, such as yours. I, myself, have been out to eight, so far this year. Clusters happen from time-to-time. They mean nothing on their own."

"Understood." Yvonne looked at Llewelyn.

He stood. "I've told Dr Jenkins he can use desk space

here whenever he needs it. It'll make liaison easier if we are all in the same building."

The DI nodded. "Sounds sensible to me."

"I won't be here every day." Jenkins brushed his trousers free of biscuit crumbs. "I can do Some stuff at home, and via phone and email, but I'll aim to be here a minimum of twice a week, if that suits?"

Yvonne shrugged. "Suits me." She looked across at the DCI.

Llewelyn nodded his agreement. "That's it, then. Yvonne, would you and Dewi like to show Dr Jenkins around?"

Yvonne was about to shake Gethin Jenkins' hand again, but changed her mind as she saw him run it through his slick comb-over. She placed hers firmly in her skirt pockets.

∽

Yvonne placed a file in front of her sergeant. "That's a copy of the witness statements from the Brecon air accident. Makes for a very interesting read."

"Why interesting?" He picked up the file.

"It involved a light aircraft and a military jet in a mid-air collision. Three witnesses reported the civilian craft circling the area where the jet came through."

"Okay..."

"The jet was a military training aircraft. It took the tail off the civilian plane in the impact. The investigation found no mechanical fault with either aircraft and there had been sufficient fuel onboard the small plane for the entirety of its flight."

"So, it wasn't looking for a landing site because of any issue?" Dewi frowned.

"There was no mayday call. The investigation concluded

that pilot error caused the accident, the fault being that of the pilot of the civilian craft."

"I see."

"Well, what if it wasn't an error? What if the small aircraft pilot knew that the military craft would come through and was waiting for it?"

"A suicide mission? Really? That's a bit of a stretch, Yvonne."

"Maybe."

Dewi shook his head. "Those military jets go a helluva lick. How would a light aircraft, relying on visual cues only, be in the right place at the right time to cause a collision with a jet flying at speed?"

"With great difficulty, but what if they had repeated attempts at getting in the way and that time they got lucky?" Yvonne pointed at the file. "One witness reported seeing a very similar light airplane doing exactly the same manoeuvres during the week before and, possibly, also during the two weeks before that. The witness is a farmer who, I understand, is out on the land a lot when those jets come through. I would very much like to speak with him. There were no other witnesses to the previous sightings and, in gathering evidence, the investigation disregarded the farmer's suggestion that hanging about was a behavioural habit of the civilian craft."

"Okay, I'll look at the file." Dewi pulled at his lower lips. "It's an intriguing case, if the farmer was right about the airplane regularly hanging about in that area. Why was his testimony disregarded?"

"He couldn't be sure that the aircraft involved in the collision was the same one he had seen previously. He thought it had the same markings, but couldn't swear to it. Several light aircraft use that airspace, so they couldn't use his statement as evidence for very much. It's tantalising, though. My gut tells me something's off. Whatever Gethin Jenkins says about statistical clusters."

"I have a lot of respect for your gut." Dewi laughed. "I'll give this a read and let you know what I think."

4
PARALLEL LINES

Yvonne perused all the information they had on the pilots of the Welshpool crash.

In one plane, a pilot and passenger both lost their lives. The other plane was solo-occupied, and that pilot also died in the collision.

Keith Files had been a pilot for fifteen years and flown both single-engine aircraft and gliders. His passenger, Philip Nugent, had been up with Files many times and twice before, that month.

Files had left a wife and two young daughters, aged six- and eight years old.

Nugent was unmarried and training to be a pilot.

In the other plane, the solo pilot was a Mathew Roberts. He'd had his pilot's licence for only four years, but had clocked up an impressive two hundred flight hours in that time, so was hardly lacking in experience.

"It's not a lot, ma'am, I know," Callum said of his notes. "But we're organising interviews with family members and, when we're finished, we'll know a lot more. Post Mortem results should be with us in the next twenty-four hours." He tilted his head, examining the DI's pensive expression.

"It's okay. It's good, Callum. You're doing great work. Make sure we get a copy of the results from toxicology, too. If there was anything in the systems of these pilots, I want to know about it, ASAP."

"Yes, ma'am."

"Looks like the oldest occupant of the planes was the family man, Keith Files, at forty-three. The other pilot was twenty-nine and Files' passenger was twenty-two."

Callum nodded. "Makes a cardiac event less likely." He shrugged.

"Yeah. Let's see what the pathologist says. In the meantime, can you tell Dewi I need the phone number of Carl Evans at Ty Newydd farm, near Brecon? He witnessed a crash between a military jet and a light aircraft. He thought the plane was lying in wait for the jet. That's not what the investigation found, but I'd still be interested in talking to him, given what one of our witnesses said about Keith Files' airplane, appearing to target Mathew Roberts' plane. It may be something and nothing, but..."

"I'm on it, ma'am." Callum turned on his heel, his long mac catching the arm of an office chair, sending it tumbling to the floor.

∽

THE HOUSE LOOKED dark and empty. Cold. Yvonne switched off the engine of her car and stared at the lonely facade, drumming up enthusiasm to go inside.

She had gotten used to the porch lights being on at night; the house lit up and warmed for when she came home. Mid-October had set in, along with a rapid fall in temperature.

It was almost two weeks since Tasha had left for London, and the DI missed her. She would be back before long, but that thought did not assuage the numbing solitude.

Her walk to the front door took twice as long as it usually did. She put her bags down and stared at the night sky, gazing at the stars of the milky way, through clouds of her own breath, allowing herself to wonder at it. It comforted her to think, perhaps, Tasha was looking up, at that very moment, too. She resolved to text the psychologist as soon as she had settled inside.

It took a while to get the fire going. The wood had gotten damp. She scrunched copious pages of the County Times to get it going.

About to rip out another page, Yvonne stopped to look at the image on it. Bits of plane, smoke from smouldering clumps of mangled metal, and a muddied shoe in a field. The photo was of the Welshpool crash site. The article asked why the police had made so little progress in their investigation into the cause of the crash, like two weeks would be enough to have all the answers.

In the background, stood the fire engines, and ambulances for which there had been little use on the day, life having been extinct for some time in the burned and broken bodies of the crash zone.

The DI ran her hand over the photo as though to comfort the victims, victims whose families she would begin questioning the following day. She didn't scrunch up that page. It didn't seem right. In her mind's eye, she saw her husband's glider slam into parked cars at Sherbourne, felt again the panic and fear, saw her husband's mangled glider engulfed in flame, remembered holding his hand as he lay dying in hospital. A solitary tear tracked its way down her cheek. It tightened her resolve for answers.

As the wood cracked in the fireplace, its warmth permeated her, lifting her out of the melancholy into which she had descended, she promised a myriad unseen loved ones she would root out the cause of the Welshpool disaster.

5

A CURIOUS DISCLOSURE

Dewi sat alone, eating an egg sandwich, studying the crash scene photographs.

Yvonne wanted to tell him about Tasha before speaking to anyone else. She felt gradual disclosure best.

"Dewi."

"Ma'am, I thought I'd get my lunch in, now, while I have the chance."

"Good idea." There followed an awkward silence, Yvonne chewing on the inside of her cheek.

"Are you okay?" he asked as she moved closer, shifting her weight between her feet.

She cleared her throat. "There's something I've been meaning to talk to you about."

Dewi turned to face her fully, setting his half-eaten sandwich down on the desk, his expression, soft. "What's up? You're looking pained." His eyes searched her face, his head tilting as he waited.

"How's your wife?" It blurted forth. Not the words she wanted, but something to fill the gap. Something to push back her nerve-wracking disclosure, the imminence of which had stiffened her jaw and dried her throat.

Dewi's frown lines deepened. "My wife? You wanted to talk about my wife?"

Yvonne forced a light air. "Yes. You haven't mentioned her recently, and I was just... wondering how she was?"

Dewi chuckled. "Are you feeling all right?"

She flicked her head. "Of course I am, why?"

"Because you're acting strange and you've got perspiration on your forehead."

She wiped a hand across her head, looking at her fingers to examine how much of the traitorous sweat had leaked. "I'm hot," she said, finally.

"Well, you're the only one in the station who is. The boiler went on the blink and we've got no heating, just as the weather has taken a turn for the worse. I have requested engineers, but they won't be here until this afternoon."

She pulled a face. "I'm hot because I've been busy."

"Well, since you're here, look at these." Dewi slid several crash scene photographs towards her. "There was an unbelievably large search area for the debris from those small aircraft."

Yvonne nodded. "What, am I looking at?"

"I got hold of all the photos from the Brecon incident. You know, the military plane smashing into the light aircraft. The one where the farmer felt the small plane had been hanging around for a while."

"I know. I intend interviewing the farmer."

"Yeah, well, six people lost their lives that day. One victim fell onto a garage roof." Dewi grimaced. "Imagine walking out of your house to find a body on top of your shed."

Yvonne shuddered. "Poor sod... The dead man, I mean, not the householder, although I feel sorry for them, too."

"I've organised an interview with the farmer." Dewi tapped his notebook. "This afternoon, at two-thirty."

Yvonne checked her watch. "Great, that gives us plenty of time to get there."

"Get there? I thought you wanted to do it by phone?"

"Yes, well, I've changed my mind. I'd like to see where it happened and talk to Carl Evans in person."

"It's not our jurisdiction."

"Yes, but I can argue a link."

"Right you are, ma'am. I'd better let him know."

∽

THE RAIN HELD OFF, for now.

Yvonne threw her mac onto the back seat of the car as Dewi got into the driver's side. She was happy to be the passenger while her thoughts about the case cast a haze over her consciousness.

The myriad Autumn colours of the Powys countryside blurred by as they drove the one-and-a-half hours to Brecon.

Carl Evans' sheep farm lay between Brecon and Sennybridge, at the edge of the Brecon Beacons National Park.

Not for the first time, Yvonne mused that in another life she would have happily been a farmer, working this breathtaking landscape, surrounded by animals mewing. A landscape so sparsely populated that astronomers flocked from all over the world to marvel at its night skies, there being no light pollution.

Both the DI and Dewi donned wellingtons before trudging through the farmyard to find Mr Evans.

"Ready?" Dewi slammed the car boot shut.

"Let's go." Yvonne strode towards the building, making use of the hood on her mac as the rain finally came, pelting the muddied concrete in front of them.

A broad-shouldered male, around six feet in height, wearing a flat cap and a khaki body warmer over a flannel shirt, approached them from the direction of the red-brick outbuildings with his sleeves rolled up.

"Carl Evans?" Yvonne asked, holding out her hand.

He wiped both of his down the front of his muddy jeans before accepting her offered one and giving it a firm shake. "That's me. I hope you don't mind the state I'm in. It's been crazy-busy and no time to clean up, yet." He pulled a face.

The DI smiled. "It's no problem. You're a busy man. We know the feeling."

He looked older than his fifty years, his face well-lined.

She pointed to the buildings. "Shall we go somewhere dry?"

"Oh, sorry, yes." He led the way across the rest of the yard to a thick-framed oak door, leading into a kitchen, the warmth of which was a welcome pleasure to the two detectives.

On the feeling the heat hit her back, Yvonne gave a shudder. She hadn't realised how cold and damp she was.

Carl Evans' kitchen was huge. The sort you might expect in a large farmhouse. The heat came from a solid fuel range.

The farmer poured from a pot into the mugs. "That's tea," he said. "I made it ten minutes ago. Help yourselves to the sugar and milk."

He pointed to a striped jug and pot in the middle of the table where they had seated themselves. "There's fruitcake, if you want some."

Yvonne shook her head. "Not for me, thank you."

Dewi's face lit up. "Love a bit of fruitcake. I'll have a slice off you, boy."

Carl grinned at him. "My sister made it. She's a fairly good cook, mind."

The DI helped herself to milk. "Mr Evans-"

"Carl. I feel odd being called Mr Evans."

"Thank you, Carl. You know we're here to talk to you about the air-collision you witnessed two months ago between a light aircraft and a jet."

Carl finished his mouthful of cake and washed it down with a swig of tea. "Helluva thing, it was. Bit surreal, like. I saw the jet come in low and fast. I could see the airplane right in its path, and I watched the jet smack right into it, a good second or so before I heard the bang. The small plane went into a tailspin. Terrible, it was. And the military jet was oozing fuel from its wings as it fell."

"I see."

"It smashed into the hillside and exploded. Broken plane and glass landed everywhere and there were a few small fires, here and there." He shook his head. "We went out there, after calling the emergency services. We found only bodies. No survivors. One body was badly burned. You couldn't have recognised him."

"Was that someone from the jet?"

"Yes, it was. The small plane came down further on, close to a cottage. The pilot of that plane landed on the shed next to the cottage, and the plane hit the ground and not the house, thankfully."

"Thank goodness." Yvonne pursed her lips. "You told the investigation you thought the airplane had been hanging around as though waiting for the jet to come through, and that you believed you'd seen it around that area frequently, during the time leading up to the accident."

Carl rubbed his grey stubble. "I did. I'm sure I did, except I couldn't exactly describe markings on the plane. The look of it, and the sound of the engine... I'm sure in my own mind it was the same plane. I just couldn't swear to that under oath like they wanted me to."

"How was the plane behaving in the sky?"

"The Cessna?"

"Yes."

"It was circling. Not large circles, like you sometimes see the sight-seeing crafts do, taking pictures or something. They were tight circles as though they wanted to hold position."

"How often were the military jets coming through here?"

"Oh, two or three times a week. I don't know if it's anything to do with it, but there's army at Sennybridge. I think the jets are American."

Yvonne wrote a few notes. "How many times would you say you saw the small plane during the preceding weeks?"

"Five or six at least."

"In the same place?"

"Pretty much, yes."

"What about before that?"

"Well, I only noticed it over that one-month period. I didn't notice any planes hanging around before that time."

"And you would have seen it, had it been there?"

"I'm sure I would have. I'm always out and about on the land."

"Did you ever see anything drop from the plane? Any vehicles approaching it?"

"No."

"Would you take us to the crash site?"

"Well, it's all cleared up now. Not much to see compared with two months ago."

"I know." Yvonne nodded. "I should still like to see it, if possible."

"Now?" Evans rose from his seat.

"That would be great."

"We'll go in my land rover."

6
ACCIDENT BY DESIGN

Two months had passed since the collision, but when she saw crash site for herself, she realized how ordinary the area now appeared.

Six people lost their lives that day, two in the light aircraft and four in the military jet, and there was little sign that anything had happened, save for the singular gouge in the hillside where the jet impacted and a few singed areas of grass. Though the rain had stopped, the moody sky lent a sombre air to scene.

Animals grazed, grass grew, and the world moved on. A singular bunch of dried-up roses lay at the foot of the hill, next to the burrowed soil. A lump clogged Yvonne's throat. Not much to mark the passing of those lives.

"Do you still need me? Only, I've got lots I need to get on with." Evans blinked at her and she saw an empathy in those weather-worn eyes.

"Of course. If we could have a lift back to the farm, we'll be on our way. I appreciate you giving us your time as you have done today."

As they got back to their own vehicle, Dewi frowned. "If it was the same plane on all those occasions, what was it doing? Surely the pilots couldn't have wanted that accident to happen, could they? A suicide mission? I don't buy it."

"It's odd." Yvonne gazed across the grassy landscape. "I'd like to speak to Gethin Jenkins, again, and a guy called Tim Payne."

"Tim Payne?" Dewi raised his eyebrows.

"Hmm. Ryan Aston, a witness to the Welshpool crash, said he has an experienced light aircraft pilot as a friend. That's Payne. I think he could be of help to us."

"Isn't that what the AAIB inspectors are for?"

"Payne will know the Powys air spaces very well, and things like local weather, air traffic control, etc. I know we could get all that from the AAIB, but Payne will know this area better. I know nothing about light aircraft travel and not much about air travel, full stop. I need to change that, and fast."

7

MISSING FILES

Mrs Cynthia Files stared wide-eyed at the DI as she opened the door.

Yvonne narrowed her eyes, "DI Giles. Sorry, were you not expecting me?"

Cynthia looked down as though trying to remember, her unkempt blonde hair falling over her face. The DI recognised the signs. This was someone going over and over her loved one's last moments. The last time they had spoken. The last time they had interacted. Wondering if she could have said or done something different. Something that could have prevented the inevitable. Grief did that to a person.

The DI's heart went out to her. "Shall I come back another time?" she asked, her voice soft.

Cynthia looked up, the confusion in her eyes lessening as though she was returning to the present. "No, don't go. Come in. I'm sorry, everything's..."

Yvonne glanced at the discarded coats, clothing, and dirty plates. She understood. "Don't worry about that. I can help, if you like. I'll take the dishes out for you."

Mrs Files made no objection, but followed as the DI she examined every doorway until she found the kitchen.

"Are you alone here?"

Cynthia nodded.

"Do you have people checking on you? Supporting you?"

Cynthia nodded again. "Martin, my son is here most evenings. He's in college in the day. He'll be back later. It's better when he's here. I still feel... lost."

"Of course." Yvonne rubbed Cynthia's elbow. "I came to talk to you about Keith and how he was in the weeks leading up to the accident."

"What do you mean?" Cynthia's wide eyes narrowed, scrutinising the DI's face. Her own, appeared gaunt. Haunted.

"We're still trying to establish the cause of the collision, Mrs Files. To date, the investigation has found no mechanical fault."

"Wait, are you implying that my husband felt depressed? That he caused the accident on purpose?" Cynthia put a hand to her forehead, her mouth open.

"No, no, I promise I am not making assumptions. I'm asking, so that we can establish whether he was in good health, physically and mentally, and whether there was anything affecting him during his last few months. I didn't mean to cause offence."

Cynthia blanched. "I'm sorry, DI Giles. I'm not myself. I miss him. He should be with me, not lying on a slab."

"I know." Yvonne pressed her lips together, tilting her head.

"I didn't notice anything different about him. He didn't mention any concerns, or health problems, to me."

"Had he visited his GP at all?"

"No. Not for years. At least, that I know of."

"What did he do, besides flying?"

"He ran a local computer repair shop with Philip."

"Was that Philip Nugent? His passenger that day?"

Cynthia nodded. "Phil had worked at the shop for a year, or so, before he started flying with Keith. Then, once he'd been up with my husband, that was it. He wanted to learn to fly the planes, himself. It thrilled Keith that he could take someone up as enthusiastic as he was. The pair of them were like kids in a toy shop, around planes."

"Did he have any other hobbies? Your husband, I mean."

"He pottered in the garden a bit. Other than that, it was reading about flying on the web, or playing with his flight simulator set-up."

"Flight simulator?"

"Uh huh."

"Can I see it?"

Cynthia rose from her seat. "Sure, it's in the attic. He used the attic as his study for all things aeronautical. I showed it to the other gentleman, yesterday."

Yvonne frowned. "What gentleman do you mean?"

"Er, Jenkins? I think that's what he said his name was."

"Do you mean Gethin Jenkins, the accident investigations guy?"

"From the AAIB, yes. They are coming to remove the stuff, later today."

Yvonne wrote herself a note to speak to Jenkins.

Cynthia led her up two flights of stairs, to the town house attic, a converted room with a skylight window.

There were three large computer monitors, a hard drive, a keyboard and joysticks. Someone had covered them with transparent plastic and taped them up, ready for removal. A leather swivel chair faced the set up, over the back of which someone had placed a headset.

"How much time did he spend up here, Mrs Files?"

"Oh, two to three hours most evenings. Sometimes, more. Often, he would get into bed well past midnight."

"I see. Did he always use his simulator on his own?"

"No. Phil used to join him regularly. They'd take it in turns controlling it. I would pop in with the occasional cuppa but, other than that, I left them to it."

"What sort of flights did they simulate?"

Cynthia shrugged. "I couldn't tell you. Like I say, I left them to it. You could look at the saved missions on the memory sticks. That gentleman, Jenkins, took them with him when he left, yesterday."

"Right." Yvonne made another note. "What about the hard drive, itself?" Yvonne pointed to the setup.

"He kept nothing on the hard drive. At least, there was nothing saved." Cynthia stated.

"Nothing at all?"

"That Jenkins guy said their engineers would be back for it today. He said I was not to touch it in the meantime. That's why it's all taped up. He took a quick look and told me the drive was empty."

"I see." Yvonne frowned. "Don't worry, I'll be speaking to him this week. I'll ask him about it."

"I'm sorry, Inspector, I ought to make a start on my son's dinner. Is there anything else you'd like to speak to me about?"

Yvonne shook her head. "Not at the moment, no." She gave Mrs Files her card. "Call me if you think of anything else. Anything at all, okay?"

"All right." Cynthia accepted the card and led the DI down the stairs, pausing at the bottom. "If you find out why it happened, you will tell me, won't you?"

Yvonne nodded. "Of course."

LLEWELYN POURED HIMSELF A COFFEE. "Ah, Yvonne. I've been looking for you," he greeted her, eyes bright.

She thought of the bags under her own eyes, the ones she had analysed in the mirror while smothering them in vitamin E cream. "Sir?"

"Gethin Jenkins is coming in today. I thought you might like to know. How is the investigation coming along?"

She pursed her lips. "It is progressing, but not as fast as I would like."

"Dewi tells me you went to Brecon yesterday." His eyes narrowed. "Was that strictly necessary?"

She kept her tone firm and even. "Yes. Absolutely. I wanted to see a crash site for myself and speak to a witness in person."

"Why?"

"To assess his credibility. There are significant parallels between a collision that happened there and ours at Welshpool."

Llewelyn rubbed the stubble on his chin. "And, what were your conclusions?"

"That the witness was credible and that his testimony puts me in significant doubt of the AAIB findings on that case."

Llewelyn loosened his tie, casting his eyes over his shoulder. "Not so loud. He'll be here any minute. Besides, you know decisions cannot rest on heresy evidence. If that witness had sworn to his facts, there might have been a different outcome. As it is, he wasn't sure enough and questioning an official body's findings without solid testimony is a precarious business."

"But, what if he was right? What if we have two collisions committed with intent? What could have made that happen? The Welshpool crash took place on a clear, cloudless, windless afternoon. Why did one of those planes fly so erratically when, at least to date, they've found no mechanical fault? I'm still waiting for the autopsy results, but early indications were that there was nothing physically wrong with the occupants of either of the planes."

"The autopsy results are on your desk."

"What?" She raised her eyebrows. "Well, great."

"I took a quick look." Llewelyn pulled a face. "I hope you don't mind. All the victims appeared to be in good health and toxicology came up negative."

Yvonne frowned, scratching her head. "No drugs or alcohol?"

"Go see for yourself."

∽

Sure enough, all three of their victims were fit, and no injuries or substance misuse was detected.

"Perhaps, I should interview Ryan Aston again. Ask him how sure he is of what he told me. If his description of the collision was a true reflection of events, then either Keith Files or his passenger Philip Nugent wanted themselves and others, dead. The question is, why?"

Llewelyn shrugged. "I agree. Speak to your witness. Find out if he was sober when he saw what he thinks he saw and find out if he had any reason to mislead you. Get him to go over the events again."

Yvonne was about to leave, when Gethin Jenkins appeared in the office. Blue shadows lurked beneath his eyes.

"Hello, Gethin." Yvonne noted the dark lines. "Can I have a word?"

He paused, a file tucked under his arms, his eyes scrutinizing her face. "Is it important?" He checked his watch.

"It is, actually. Yes."

"Very well."

Yvonne tilted her head. "You look tired. Late night?"

He paled, loosening his tie as he walked towards her. "I couldn't sleep. Just couldn't get comfortable."

The DI rubbed her lip with her thumb. "I went to see Cynthia Files, earlier."

His eyes jerked to hers. "Oh?"

"She told me you'd been to see her, and that you had taken some memory sticks belonging to her late husband, containing files from his simulator."

He cleared his throat with a grunt. "Yes, I did."

"Are we allowed to know what is on those sticks?"

He shook his head. "You could have, but someone has wiped them clean."

"Who?"

"Well, presumably Keith Files."

"Where are they now?"

"They are on their way to our labs in Farnborough. The engineers will see if there is anything they can retrieve from them."

"I don't understand."

"Someone reformatted them." Jenkins' tone was matter-of-fact.

"Why would Keith Files have done that?"

He shrugged. "Your guess is as good as mine. You know, he may just have refreshed everything. Mrs Files explained that he recently upgraded the software on the simulator. He may have started everything afresh. Perhaps, the new software couldn't read the old files."

Yvonne frowned. It did not sit right. She stared at Jenkins, sure there was something he wasn't telling her. "If Farnborough find anything, would you let me know?" She forced a lightness to her tone, her face softening to a smile which did not quite reach her eyes.

"Of course." He nodded without smiling, the muscles in his face, tense. The knuckles of his hand were white as they gripped the file.

8

UNEXPECTED DEVELOPMENTS

Callum and Dai grabbed her at the top of the station stairs.

She stopped to catch her breath. "Hello, you two. What's so urgent?"

"Just found out something very interesting, ma'am." Callum checked his notes. "Philip Nugent, Keith Files' passenger, was engaged to one Michaela Harris. The lady in question lives in Builth Wells. Miss Harris is pregnant, it would appear, with his child."

"Really?" Yvonne frowned. "Oh, the poor girl."

"But, here's the thing." Dai's eyes shone. "Six weeks before he died, Nugent took out a personal insurance on himself for six hundred thousand pounds, payable to Miss Harris, on his death. Interesting timing, don't you think?" Dai finished with a deep breath.

Yvonne nodded. "I'd say it's very interesting. Perhaps, we should talk to this Miss Harris. Do you have an address?"

"We do."

"Get in touch with her and set up an appointment. Let's see what she has to say." Yvonne sighed. "I should think it might interest the insurance company, too. It could be an innocent coincidence, but the timing leaves us with important questions, for sure."

"We'll get it set up, ma'am."

"Thanks."

∼

TASHA THREW her bag down in the hall and rushed through to find the DI in the kitchen, putting away the clean dishes from the dishwasher.

Yvonne swung around. "You're back!" She tossed the tea towel onto the drainer and ran to hug the psychologist. "I missed you."

Tasha's smile lit her whole face. "I missed you, too. We haven't finished in London. I have to go back next week, but I couldn't wait that long to see you again."

The DI grinned at her. "You are such a softie, but I am so glad to see you. Just don't wear yourself out, going back and forth. I need to know you are looking after yourself and we can always face-time, if needs be."

"Yes, but face-time won't let me do this." Tasha hugged her tight.

Yvonne coughed as the air was squeezed out of her.

Relenting, the psychologist slackened her grip, but continued to hold her partner for several moments, gently rocking her from side-to-side.

"So, how's the case going in London?" Yvonne asked, eventually.

"It's moving along, but nowhere near fast enough for the commissioner." Tasha grimaced. "I can't say too much. They have sworn me to secrecy."

"Really?" Yvonne stared at her, wide-eyed.

"Well, not really, but it is sensitive, so-"

Yvonne held up a hand. "It's okay, don't say anymore."

"What about you? How's yours progressing?"

Yvonne sighed. "Don't ask. According to the AAIB, there's likely no case to answer though, despite that, they appear to be taking a keen interest."

"I see."

The DI brushed a stray hair from her face. "Anyway, are you up for lamb tagine? I've got one cooking in the oven."

Tasha placed her hands on her hips. "Am I ready? For lamb tagine? Are you kidding? Let me at it."

∾

Yvonne drummed her fingers on the steering wheel, waiting for the lights to change. She grunted, a forty-five minute journey had already taken an hour and ten minutes. Perking up as the lights changed to amber, she put her foot down, not waiting for green.

As she pulled alongside Llyn Clywedog, otherwise known as Clywedog Dam, she spotted several emergency service vehicles already on site. Three ambulances, two fire engines and four or five police vehicles. She scoured the roadway for Dewi, spotting him in conversation with a police diver.

"No survivors, I'm afraid, ma'am." He shook his head as she caught up with him. "Both planes or, rather, the pieces of them, are in there." He pointed at the dam.

"Do we know who was in them?" she asked, her eyes skimming the surfaces as though she might see the wreckage beneath.

"Not yet."

"Who called it in?"

Dewi pointed to a couple further along the shore, blankets around their shoulders; uniformed officers taking their statements.

Dewi ran a hand through his hair. "They know nothing, apart from what they witnessed, which was two planes colliding over the dam. They said they didn't see the collision itself. They saw the first plane come in, before they turned away to get their picnic food out of the car boot. They heard the second plane's engine and then the bang, which they said made them jump out of their skins. They ducked behind their car, as the bits rained down."

"Did you record what they said?" She asked, pointing to his body camera.

"I did."

"Good work." She sighed, rubbing the back of her neck. "What the hell is going on?"

"Your guess is as good as mine, but something's not right."

"You can say that again." Her gaze took in the deep plums, ochres and russets of leaves in their final bloom. She mused that, for whoever was flying those planes, that colourful display was one of the last things they would have seen.

The diver, Dewi had been talking to earlier, approached them. His colleagues were still in the lake, appearing and disappearing every so often.

He nodded to Yvonne. "No survivors confirmed. We will need specialist equipment to get to the wreckage. Worst place for it to have happened, for the recovery team."

Yvonne nodded. "Did you see anything?"

He shook his head. "One of our divers has a camera. He got some footage through the murk kicked up by the debris.

We will organise the recovery, once the AAIB give us the go ahead. One of their guys is on his way over."

"Very well." Yvonne straightened her skirt. "I guess we'll know who the victims are, soon enough. I want to hear as soon as you know anything."

A shout went up from the dam.

Dewi peered to see what was happening as two divers appeared from the lake, holding something between them, which they began loading onto a red search-and-rescue dinghy. "Looks like a body, ma'am."

Yvonne grimaced. "Such a sad business. I can't believe it, coming so soon after the Welshpool crash." She motioned her DS. "Come with me. I want to visit Philip Nugent's fiancé. Apparently, he took out a hefty insurance policy shortly before he died. She's the beneficiary. Let's see what she has to say about his death."

"Right, you are."

9

AFFAIRE DE COEUR

Michaela Harris answered the door in her dressing gown, her shoulder-length blonde hair, unkempt. Red-eyed, she appeared to have forgotten the detectives were coming and stared at them, a glazed expression in her wide eyes.

Yvonne tilted her head, her own expression, soft. "Are you okay? Would you prefer us to come back another time?"

Michaela sniffed. "No, it's all right. I'm sorry, it's everything that has happened... Time just..."

"We understand." Yvonne smiled and placed a hand on Michaela's arm "You've had a horrible shock, one that would put anyone's head in a spin. You don't have to explain."

Michaela nodded and stepped back to allow them in.

"Is the baby all right?" The DI asked, as she took a seat in the lounge of the terraced house in Builth.

Michaela nodded. "I had another scan, yesterday, and all looks well. I bled a bit, after I heard the news about Phil. That was very scary. My parents took me to the hospital. I was so afraid I would lose both of them in the same day." She hung her head.

"Did you go to Shrewsbury hospital?"

Michaela shook her head. "Telford."

"It's a long way to go, when you are fearing for your child. I'm glad everything was okay. Do you mind if I ask you some questions about Philip?"

"No, go ahead." Michaela wiped the back of her hand across her eyes.

"My sergeant is wearing a body camera. I that okay?"

The woman straightened her hair. "Yes, that's fine." She looked down at her clothes and grimaced.

"It's okay, the film is for our records, so we miss nothing."

"Okay." Michaela put her hands together in her lap, the fingers intertwined as though comforting themselves.

"Miss Harris, how was Philip in the weeks leading up to the crash? Was he in good health?"

The young woman nodded. "He was healthy as far as we know and fit." Michaela glanced from Yvonne, to Dewi, and back. "He went to the gym most evenings for an hour. He hadn't visited a GP for a while."

"What about mentally? Was he happy?"

Michaela's eyes travelled to the window and the row of houses opposite. "The news about the baby thrilled him. I've never seen him happier, but..."

"But?" Yvonne kept her voice gentle.

"He'd had depression about two years ago, when he lost a job he loved. They made him redundant. It was a case of last in and first out. He was young, and it was his first job. It took him a while to come out the other side. He was on the tablets for about six months." Michaela pursed her lips. "Emotionally, he could be fragile. He lost his mother when he was twelve, to cancer, and it affected him. I don't think he ever really got over that."

"I see." Yvonne rubbed her chin. "Do you think he could have been suicidal?"

"What, now?" Michaela looked at the DI with an open mouth. "Wait, you think he caused the crash on purpose?"

"I'm just examining all possibilities." Yvonne sighed. "I'm keeping an open mind. In our job, one can't assume anything."

Michaela cast her gaze downward. "I don't know. I wouldn't have said he was down, but I have to admit that, due to my condition, he may have wanted to protect me from feelings like that, so may have kept them from me." She bit her lip. "I don't think so, though."

"Miss Harris, did Philip have any personal insurance?"

"Not that I know of."

"Are you saying that you were not aware of a six-hundred thousand pound personal insurance policy?"

"Wow, no."

"You were the main beneficiary."

Michaela's mouth fell open.

"You definitely didn't know?"

"Well, he had said to me that he might take out insurance, with a baby on the way, but he didn't tell me he had done it."

"You're saying he didn't tell you."

"Yes. That is exactly what I am saying."

With no evidence to the contrary, Yvonne had to leave it there. She shifted in her seat. Pressure had been building in her abdomen and was becoming unbearable. She wished she had been to the toilet before leaving the station. "I'm sorry, Miss Harris, might I use your bathroom?"

Michaela nodded. "Yes, of course. It's upstairs, first door on your left."

The DI took the stairs two at a time, worried in case she didn't make it.

The bathroom was small, but not uncomfortably so. The toilet was next to the bath in the grey-and-white-styled room.

Her eyes strayed to a chrome cabinet, and she pursed her lips as she pondered the fact she did not have a search warrant.

On washing her hands, she could see that the cabinet was open just two centimetres. She made the gap wider and peered inside. Toothpaste, hair gel, aftershave, eau de toilette and several small prescription packets.

Yvonne used her thumbnail to move the packets a touch, so that she could read the labels.

Three of the four was in Michaela's name. One, however, was not, A pack of anti-depressants prescribed at one per day, in the name of Philip Nugent. It was dated May of that year, so was only five months old.

The DI drew in a sharp breath. What was Michaela not telling her?

Michaela and Dewi were discussing names for the baby when Yvonne returned to the lounge.

She sat down, clearing her throat. "Thank you." Her eyes were on Michaela's face. "I'm so sorry, but as I was washing my hands, I saw a prescription packet in your cabinet."

Michaela coloured.

"Anything you want to tell me?"

"Are you talking about the anti-depressants?"

"Yes."

"Phil renewed his prescription for it, in case he had another low mood. He had a bout several months back and took the pills for about two weeks until he felt better."

"What was going on five months ago?"

Michaela shrugged. "Nothing, I know of. I think he just renewed his prescription."

Yvonne sensed there was more to it, but it was clear the information would not be forthcoming. Michaela looked like she was holding her breath. "If you remember anything relevant, you will let me know, won't you?"

"Yes." Michaela sighed. "He didn't cause that accident on purpose, you know. He wouldn't have done that. He wouldn't."

"Did he get on well with Keith Files?"

"Yes. They were best mates, even though there was a twenty-year age gap. They were like brothers, and both addicted to flying. They got on like a house on fire."

"So, they never fell out?"

"Never. Not to my knowledge, and Phil would have told me, I'm sure."

"He didn't tell you about the insurance."

"I never heard him say a bad word about Keith, and I know he really admired his flying skills."

"And how about his training to fly? Was that going well?"

"Yes. He'd always come home buzzing with excitement after going up with Keith. He hadn't quite got to the stage where he could go solo, but he would have done by the end of the year."

"I see."

"I miss him."

At least, with the last, Michaela appeared sincere, her eyes, soulful.

The DI stood. "Here is my card, Miss Harris. If you think of anything else that might be important, please call me."

Michaela nodded. "I will."

Yvonne was deep in thought as they left the house. As

she looked towards the road, she saw a black Audi and, striding towards them, was none other than Ryan Aston.

She opened her mouth to speak to him as she reached Michaela's gate, but he had turned on his heel and was heading back to the Audi.

"Mr Aston?" She called, breaking into a run.

He stopped walking, his back still to her, shoulder's stiff.

"Mr Aston? I thought I recognised you." She caught up with him as he turned to her.

"Hello, again." He stared at her, his expression, cold. "Are you following me?"

Yvonne raised her eyebrows. "We've been here a while. You have only just arrived. How could we be following you?"

He looked towards the house.

"Are you on your way to see Michaela Harris?"

"What? No. I'm..." He shrugged. "Yes."

"I didn't realise you knew her?"

"I don't. Well, not very well. I've seen her from a distance, when she was with Philip. I just came as a one-off, to offer her my condolences."

"I see. Did you know her fiancé, then?"

"Yes, I knew him but, again, not that well."

"Then, why?" She glanced at the house and thought she saw the curtains twitch.

He rubbed his cheek. "I'd seen him, occasionally, at the airport, to say hello to. I liked what I knew of him. He seemed a decent, friendly guy."

"How did you get his address?"

"I asked the owner of the airport."

"Why did you change your mind when you saw us here?"

"I only intended a quick visit. I've got stuff to do, and I thought you might keep me."

"Why?" Yvonne's eyes stayed on his face.

He shrugged. "I don't know."

"Have you been seeing Michaela?"

"What? You mean romantically? No, of course not."

"Very well, then we've no reason to keep you."

The DI stepped aside, but not before she detected relief in the drop of his shoulders as he continued towards the house.

"What are you thinking? Insurance scam? Aston, in league with her?" Dewi asked as they got into the car.

"It's possible, isn't it?" Yvonne glanced back at the house, through the driver's mirror. "I think she was expecting him. I saw the curtains going. One thing is for sure, he didn't want us to know he would see her."

"No, I don't think he did."

∼

"Where are we off to, now?" Dewi asked, as they sped along the straight between Builth and Llandrindod Wells.

"We're off to see a guy called Tim Payne. Ryan Aston knows him and, by all accounts, he is the man to talk to about all things aviation in Powys. He also knows the skies around here, and Welshpool Airport, very well."

"Righty oh," Dewi nodded. "Does he know we're coming?"

"He should do. Dai set the meeting up for me. We need to be there by two o'clock."

Dewi checked his watch. "Cutting it fine, but we ought to make it." He pulled a face. "Guess we won't lunch until late today, then."

Yvonne grimaced. "Sorry. I'll make it up to you, I promise."

"Yeah?" Dewi raised his eyebrows, rolling his eyes.

"Sure. The next lot of cheese-and-onion sandwiches will be on me."

Dewi chuckled. "I'll hold you to that."

～

TIM PAYNE MET them at the hangar in Welshpool Airport.

He was tall, easily six foot in height, with short-cropped, grey hair. Prematurely greyed, Yvonne decided, given the smoothness of his skin.

She held out her hand.

He gave it a firm, confident shake.

It was then she saw a young man looking over at them, sitting on an upturned box, drinking from a can.

"That's my son, Rob." Tim Payne jerked his head in the younger man's direction. "Seventeen and thinks he knows it all." He laughed. "Actually, he probably does."

Yvonne could see a vague resemblance, in their square chins and high foreheads. She nodded at Tim's son, who merely stared at her.

She cleared her throat.

"He doesn't say a lot until he gets to know someone," Tim apologised.

Rob put the hood up on his jacket, hands in pockets. "I got to go, now, dad. I'll see you later."

"Thank you for agreeing to see us." Yvonne cast her eyes over the small planes in the hangar. "Which one is yours?"

He pointed to a blue-and-white, single-engine Piper aircraft. "That's my main one, over there. I own it. I have access to a Cessna, too, which I jointly own with a friend. That one is out at the moment."

"I hope you don't mind, Ryan Aston gave us your name.

He suggested you as a good person to talk to about flying these skies."

Payne nodded. "That's fair. I know them as well anyone does, I guess. What can I do to help you?"

"We wanted your opinion on the accidents that have happened in the area recently. A cluster of mid-air collisions."

Tim rubbed his chin and placed both hands on the top of his head, blowing air through his teeth. "This area has had little luck of late. I've lost flying associates and friends I've known for years, like Keith Files."

"You knew him well?"

"I couldn't believe it when they said he'd smashed into another plane. I mean, I know it can happen, but rarely, and not to men like Keith."

"Has something changed recently? Traffic control systems? An increase in air traffic? Anything like that?"

He shook his head. "We're not doing anything different. We rely on visual contact and radio to avoid collisions, and that has worked very well for us, until recently. Air traffic has never been heavy enough to warrant a control tower."

"What might have gone wrong, do you think?"

He frowned. "Isn't that what yourselves and the AAIB are here to figure out?"

"Yes, but we need your input. You and people like you. It's saves us time if we have the ideas of experienced persons, like yourself. Do you have a simulator?"

"Sorry?" He jerked his head back as though it was an odd question.

"A flight simulator," she repeated. "Have you used one?"

"No, I haven't. I had access to one during my training, many years ago, but I don't use them now. I know pilots who do, however. They practice taking off and landing in difficult conditions, things like that. However, if the weather is wild, we close the airport."

"I see. Did you know that Keith Files had a simulator?"

"Did he? I didn't know that. He was an experienced pilot and a consummate professional. He loved flying. I'm not surprised he like practising in his spare time. He helped train other pilots, too. I should imagine he let them use the simulator. Plus, I can envisage him messing about with it for the sheer enjoyment, particularly on the days when the airport was closed, or he couldn't go up for whatever reason."

"So, it sounds like he never discussed using one with you."

"No, but I don't suppose there was any reason for him to."

"Do you know of anything going on in his life that might have affected his flying ability, or his concentration when he was in the air?"

"What, you mean like drugs?"

"Yes, anything like that, or anything which might have upset him, or made him feel like taking his own life?"

Tim shook his head. "Not that he ever told me."

"Can you think of any other reason an aircraft might suddenly turn and plunge into another plane? Ryan Aston stated that Keith's plane was yawing before the accident."

"Yes. That was odd. Very odd, since his aircraft got a clean bill of health earlier that same week."

"No faults?"

"None."

"Had Keith ever disclosed anything like chest pain? Visual problems?"

"No, nothing."

"Depression?"

"None, that I know of. No, wait. There was something. Over a month ago, I found him in here running a hand over his Piper. He looked like he had lost a fiver and found a penny. I joked with him about being down in the mouth, but he didn't want to talk about it. I asked him if there was a problem with the plane. He was adamant there wasn't. He said the plane was perfectly sound, and he seemed fine an hour later and I forgot all about it."

"What made you think it might be the plane?"

"Well, he was looking at it when I saw him looking sad. No other reason."

"Do you keep records of the checks?"

"Yes, we keep all paperwork, just like you would for the MOT of your car."

"And his plane had a clean bill of health?"

"Yes, like I said, the plane was in good order. No faults and no flaws."

"What does your gut tell you about the cluster of recent accidents?"

"I feel uncomfortable about it, but I cannot confirm that anything is going wrong. Unfortunately, accidents happen. We do our best to avoid them, but there you go."

Yvonne buttoned up her jacket. "We have to go, but can you contact me on this number if you think of anything else?"

"Of course." Payne took the card and placed it in the back pocket of his trousers.

"Thank you."

∽

ANOTHER DIRECT MESSAGE pinged into thirty-eight-year-old

Royston Thomas's inbox, and a smile creased the corners of his eyes.

Heart thumping, he swiped at his phone to retrieve the direct message, surprised at how quickly she had replied. She was special this one. He knew it. It was never a good idea to plan too far ahead, but still.

'I like men like you, kind and considerate.'

He put his snack down, losing his appetite to the quiver in his gut. He steadied his hand as he typed a reply. 'I like you, too.'

'Can I phone you?'

'No. Not now.' He thought of his wife, and guilt came over like a shroud, leaving a numbing ache in his forehead. Talking was fun. Meeting was something else.

He squeezed the bridge of his nose. Karen was due. She'd be here any minute.

'When?'

'I'll message you, later.'

∽

"There you are." Royston's wife, Karen, entered the hangar with their packed lunch. "You need to eat something. You'll waste away."

He accepted an offered sandwich, feeling like going into his phone and disabling his social media. "You look after me." His mouth turned down at the corners.

"What's the matter?" Karen peered into his face, concern in her narrowed eyes.

"Nothing." He slipped the phone into his pocket.

10

CUI BONO?

Callum collared Yvonne as she returned to the station. "We've got victim details for the Clywedog Dam collision, ma'am. As you know, the planes' occupants lost their lives."

Yvonne sighed, running a hand through her hair. "I know. Awful business."

"There were two victims, twenty-nine-year-old Kevin Tranchard, and thirty-six-year-old Tom Yates. Both men were experienced solo pilots." He checked his notes. "They had over four hundred flying hours, between them."

The DI pursed her lips, her eyes flicking side-to-side as she considered this. "Have we got social media profiles for the victims of this and previous crashes? If not, can you get onto it? I want them as soon as possible. I expect that's the kind of detail Gethin Jenkins looks at. Call him and see if he has that information. If he hasn't, we'll get it ourselves. If something out of the ordinary has been going on in the lives of these men, there may be clues lurking in their profiles. They may have things in common besides aviation."

"On it, ma'am." Callum made a note, underlining it twice.

"Have they pulled all the wreckage from the dam?"

"They have most of it and they estimate they'll have the rest by the end of the week."

"Great. Get copies of their preliminary findings, regarding the state of the planes prior to the crash, and do the same for the other crashes, please. I realise that the AAIB are all over this, and that they don't like to say too much until they are sure of their facts, but get what you can from Jenkins. We need something to go on. We're on borrowed time."

"Ma'am?"

"Llewelyn will want us off the investigation as soon as possible. He'll want it left to the AAIB, so we are not needlessly using resources. But, I'm not ready to hand it over, yet. Something is going on, and I want to understand what. For all we know, there could be more pilots at imminent risk."

Callum tilted his head. "Don't you trust the AAIB to get to the bottom of it?"

"It's not that. I have every respect for them, but they have limited manpower, and I strongly suspect that some sort of criminality is afoot. There are just too many coincidences, Callum. Don't you think?"

Callum shrugged, chewing the inside of his lip.

"Besides, I'm not sure Gethin Jenkins is being open with us," she whispered, casting her gaze over the open-plan office, in case he was around. "He might be, and I could be treating him unfairly, but he took a lot of computer stuff from Keith Files' house and claimed the pilot had wiped it clean. He said it's gone off to Farnborough for their forensic labs to go through it all, but... I don't know, I felt it in my gut. He was holding out on us."

"Okay."

"Can you do something else for me?"

"Sure."

"You and Dai could look into share prices of Piper and Cessna aircraft. Find someone who can tell you if anyone has been speculating on the stock market, for example, on aircraft manufacturers' shares going down in price. It's a long shot, but it's another avenue we ought to explore. If these crashes are being designed, cui bono?"

"Who benefits?" Callum played with his bottom lip, weighing up the idea.

"Yes. Who might gain from these tragedies?"

Dewi joined them with a tray of full mugs.

"Tea anyone?" He grinned.

"You are a superstar." Yvonne grinned back at him, grabbing one mug and a chocolate biscuit off the tray. "While you're here, I had a thought."

"Oh, yeah?" Dewi put the tray down on a desk.

"Don't get too excited, it's a spot of wild speculation."

"Go on."

"Well, Michaela Harris told us she's five and a half months pregnant, right?"

"Right."

"And her fiancé, Philip Nugent, renewed his anti-depressant prescription five months ago."

"You think he was unhappy about the baby?"

"It's possible. Or, perhaps, he suspected the baby wasn't his. I'm still not sure whether Ryan Aston was altruistically paying a visit to a grieving woman he barely knew, or something else. And, given the distance involved, he could hardly claim he was just passing."

"But, she has just lost her partner in a tragic incident, and Nugent was a regular at the airfield."

"Granted, but Aston tried to hide his visit from us. The question is, why? I think there is likely something going on between him and Michaela, hence my suspicion regarding the paternity of the baby."

Dewi nodded. "I agree it was suspicious, the way he turned on his heel, the minute he saw us."

"Hmm. I've asked Callum and Dai to pull together everything they can from the dead pilots' social media. Let's gather in as many pieces of this rapidly expanding jigsaw as we can."

∾

"Are you coming? I thought Llewelyn wanted to see us in his office at eleven?"

Yvonne checked her watch. "Oh, Lord, it's five-past, Dewi. Right, lead the way. I'll apologise. He'll be fine."

She straightened her skirt and blouse, clearing her throat as they reached the DCI's door.

Dewi tapped it.

"Come in."

Her eyes flicked from the DCI, to Gethin Jenkins, and back. What was he doing there, sipping from a mug; sleeves rolled up? She stared at him, open-mouthed, her stomach muscles clenching.

"Ah, Yvonne and Dewi, take a seat, would you?" Llewelyn showed them to the group of chairs alongside his desk. "I thought it would be a good time to pull together what we know about the air collisions and decide what we want to do going forward."

Yvonne clicked her tongue, noting that the DCI was in full uniform. That had to mean official business. "We're in the middle of interviewing families of the victims and the remaining witnesses, sir."

"Yes, I know. As I understand it, we have no evidence of wrongdoing. Am I right?"

The DI drew a deep breath. "As it stands, no, we don't. However, I-"

"I'm pulling you from the case."

"Sorry?"

"The end of next week, you'll officially hand over to the AAIB. They can take it from here."

"But, sir-"

He held up a hand. "No buts. We have other things to attend to, and all we are doing at the moment is duplicating each other's work. Gethin, and the AAIB engineering inspectors, are more than capable of taking this forward. There's no need for further input from us. It's a waste of resources, Yvonne. Come on, you know that."

Yvonne glanced at Dewi, then glared at the DCI and Gethin. She couldn't help it.

Llewelyn continued, "I'd like an interim report on my desk in two weeks, but you'll officially hand over, like I said, at the end of next week."

Dewi put out his hand. "I agree with Yvonne, it doesn't feel right to step back, now. It's too soon, sir. We've just uncovered important information that needs further investigation as it could be a motive for criminal behaviour."

"Such as?"

"Well, we found out that one pilot involved in the Welshpool collision had previously suffered from depression. He had renewed his anti-depressant prescription, and had taken out a substantial life insurance policy, in the weeks prior to his death. Another pilot had wiped a load of simulator files off his hard drive and memory sticks." Dewi looked to Gethin Jenkins for support on the last.

Llewelyn shrugged. "The AAIB are on it, and an insurance investigator is also on the way to look into it. We all know how tenacious *they* can be at finding the truth."

"But-"

"If Gethin and his colleagues turn up something which smells bad, we'll step back in." The DCI took a deep breath. "But, in the meantime, we're bowing out."

"Is that your final word?" Yvonne stared at him, pupils so large, her eyes appeared black. Her knuckles gleamed white as her fingernails bit into her palms.

"It is, Yvonne. I'm sorry." His face softened. "Look, I know how hard you've worked. The AAIB will use everything you've found and include it in their evidence, I'm sure. You'll get full credit."

"I don't want the credit, sir. I want answers. The victims' families deserve closure. Their loved ones died in bizarre... accidents." She gritted her teeth as she said the last. "Except, I doubt they *were* accidents. You can pull us off, now, but we'll only be back again, later. Then, we'll be having to play catch-up, instead of being fully up to speed."

"You really suspect something criminal, don't you?"

Her outburst had left her breathless. She took a moment to compose herself. "I do, yes."

"Well, if they find any criminality, Yvonne. You'll be back on the case immediately."

He had dismissed her. He would not change his mind. Further remonstration was futile. The DI didn't know whether to scream or cry. She could readily do both.

As they walked back to the main office, she spun round to Dewi. "This is Gethin's doing. I bet he's insisted on us being removed."

Dewi sighed, "Well, it's the DCI's decision. He's the one who has ultimately put the kibosh on it. But, hey, look on the bright side." He placed his tweed jacket over the back of his chair.

"What bright side?"

"We've got until the end of next week. A lot can happen in that time. We'll just keep digging."

Yvonne nodded. "Thank you for keeping me positive."

She was still working on the next week's logistics, when her DS brought her a brew, to cement that positivity.

She was about to thank him, when she spotted Jenkins, slipping into the office and switching on a PC terminal. She strode over.

As he turned, she found her face mere inches from his. "You're hiding something, I know you are. Llewelyn has taken us off the case, but I won't stop taking an interest in it, Gethin, or in you."

Gethin's forehead beaded with perspiration. He said nothing, but his hand rattled the back of the chair he was holding.

She continued. "If there is something we should know, something you buried, believe me, I will find it. I will find it, I will dig it up, and I will make it haunt you. I hope we're clear about that?"

Gethin stared at her, wide-eyed, his jaw, slack. He didn't speak. Instead, he closed his mouth, grabbed his bag, and left the office.

The fight left her with a sigh. She felt awful.

Dewi came over. "Was that wise?"

"Oh, Dewi." Her eyes filled. "I blew a fuse. I think I'm losing it."

Dewi shook his head. "You're tired. We all are. He'll get over it." He put a hand on her shoulder. "I feel your disappointment." His frown turned to a grin. "He probably deserved everything he got."

"I hate to be rude."

"You're never rude, and I'm sure you weren't rude to him. I agree, I think he went to Llewelyn to ask for the case, and you are probably right to question his motivation."

"You think?"

"Yes. No. I'm trying to help you feel better."

She laughed, despite herself. "Oh, Dewi, what would I do without you and your crap sense of humour?"

11

A VIOLENT SLAUGHTER

Yvonne tapped her pen on the desk as she waited for Jenkins to answer his phone. "Come on. Come on," she muttered. "What is taking so long?"

By the time he finally came on the line, she had drifted off in her thoughts, and the sound of his voice made her jump. "Gethin, It's Yvonne Giles. There's something I've been meaning to ask you."

"Is it important? I'm busy right now." His voice cracked. He sounded scared, irritated, or both.

"It's about the memory sticks belonging to Keith Files."

"What about them?"

"You said you thought Files had wiped them, perhaps intending to kill himself, because he didn't want his suicide to impact his wife and any insurance policy he had."

"Yes, that's what I was thinking."

She knew Jenkins was holding his breath on the other end. "Keith Files didn't have an insurance policy. He never took one out. The only money going to his wife is his works pension and lump sum."

"I know. Is that all?"

"What other reason might he have had to wipe his computer history? I mean, if his intention was suicide, he had no reason to care what was on the memory sticks, surely?"

"I don't know. Perhaps, he had been seeing someone else, and didn't want his wife hurt?"

"Then why save anything to do with his affair on the memory sticks in the first place? I thought you said he labeled them as flight simulator files. There's no reason to think they would have had personal stuff on them, is there?"

"Well, they're with Farnborough, now. We'll see what they can pull off of them." He groaned as though pained.

Yvonne frowned. "Gethin? Are you all right?"

He sighed. "There is more I could tell you, but not on the phone. I need to talk to you in person, make sure you know where I'm coming from when I explain."

"Really? Why?"

"So, you understand. Can you meet me?"

"Where are you?"

"I'm in Builth Wells. I stopped to pick up a few things from the shop, after visiting the crash site at the Dam. I will be back in Newtown this afternoon. Is there somewhere we could go? And, I'd prefer it if you came alone."

Yvonne thought about it. "All right. Meet me at the Bank Tearooms at three." She gave him directions.

Her forehead creased in concentration as she clicked her phone off. What was so important, that he needed to see her face-to-face? What had he been up to?

∽

GETHIN TOSSED the empty sandwich carton into a bin, as he strolled next to the river. He ate his lunch to the sound of gurgling water, to clear his head and get his story straight. DI Giles was an astute woman. She would see right through him.

Whichever way he cut it, it would not reflect well on him. He wondered, as he had many times before, if he could have done anything differently. Handled it better. Done the decent thing.

His mobile vibrated in his jacket pocket, then rang for good measure. He pulled it out, staring at the screen. It was them. He thought about throwing it in the river, but refrained.

"Jenkins." He wasn't aware of the figure in dark clothing, approaching along the path behind. "I won't do it. I can't do this anymore. It's gotten way out of hand. You will carry on causing deaths, and for what? It's not a game. I don't care what you do to me. I am out of this. Do you hear me? Do your worst."

As he pressed the phone off, he heard the water lapping, echoing on the underside of the bridge where the light played in kaleidoscopic patterns, reflecting off the water.

He caught the glint of something else.

A flash.

A blur.

And, he was bleeding out, hands grabbing at his neck to stem the blood.

He saw the back of his assailant as the latter fled, but he couldn't shout. Could only gurgle. He collapsed where he stood, unable to move. Unable to cry for help.

12

SHOCK

"Ma'am. You... I..." Dai struggled to find the words. His forehead creased. He placed his hands on his head, fingers entwining his hair. "You won't believe this." He sighed.

"Believe what? What's happened?" She crossed the floor in CID, grabbing his arm. "Dai?"

He took his hands down. "It's Jenkins, the AAIB inspector. He's dead."

"What?" Yvonne stared at him, wide-eyed, mouth open. "Dead? How? Where?"

"They found him under a bridge in Builth Wells. Someone cut his throat."

Yvonne grabbed the mobile radio and turned it up. "How long ago, Dewi? I spoke to him, not forty minutes ago."

Dewi shrugged. "A jogger found him. It's coming through, now. I've got a DC from Llandod on the phone for you, if you want to speak to him. He's at the scene."

"No. Tell him we're on our way. And, Dewi? Say I don't mean to be rude, I just need to get there."

"Understood, ma'am."

Yvonne grabbed her coat and bag, as Dewi finished the call. "Let's go. We'll use lights and sirens. I want to be there, yesterday."

"I'll grab my jacket, looks like we'll have a downpour any minute."

As they ran through the carpark to their unmarked vehicle, Yvonne looked up as the heavens opened. A ripping crack of thunder tore through the sky.

"This won't be fun to drive in." Dewi's breath whistled through pursed lips as he turned the car onto the main road. The rain bounced off the tarmac ahead. The windscreen wipers barely coped.

"Forget the lights and sirens." Yvonne sighed. "Take it steady. We'll get there soon enough."

Fortunately, the roads were relatively clear for most of the winding journey through the hills.

The rain lightened, too, as they reached the half-way point.

"Lucky for us, the crime scene is under a bridge," Dewi said, frowning in concentration. "That should give us extra protection from this storm."

As they pulled into the car park alongside the river in Builth, the DI threw off her seatbelt, hands shaking as she clutched her bag. Her last words to Gethin rang in her tortured mind.

She had little time to dwell. As they approached the bridge, several police and SOCO personnel were hard at work inside the cordons.

"DC Ian Rhys." A slim, young man in a leather jacket held out his hand to Dewi. "CID, Llandod."

Dewi shook the offered hand, introducing himself and Yvonne.

"I understand you knew him." Ian Rhys took a step back, allowing them a view through to the bridge, where officers in plastic suits waited for the photographer to finish.

She nodded. "He was the local AAIB inspector. He'd been helping us with a case." As she said the words, she mused at how death changed the way one described a person.

"Poor bugger couldn't have seen it coming." DC Rhys pulled a face. "It's not easy to see, through the blood, but there doesn't appear to be any defensive cuts."

Yvonne grimaced. "Perhaps, the attacker came from behind. Gethin said would meet me in Newtown this afternoon. This must have happened just before he set off."

The three detectives approached the cordon, flashed their warrant cards, and scene-watch nodded them through to suit up.

The DI tapped the shoulder of one of the SOCOs. "Did the victim have anything on him? Do you have his phone?"

The officer shook her head. "Both his phone and his wallet are absent, but we found a small notebook in his inside jacket pocket."

"May I see it?" Yvonne asked, snapping a pair of purple latex gloves.

"Sure." The officer pointed to an evidence bag. "You'll have to break the seal, and re-bag it when you've finished. Oh, yes, and sign the paperwork to say that's what you've done."

"Of course." Yvonne nodded.

Inside the notebook, Gethin had scribbled rough drawings of crash scenes and the dates and times he had spoken to people. On the last page, he had written 'Hand of Darkness', and underlined this three times.

"Hand of Darkness? That sounds a little sinister," Yvonne said out loud. "What is that?"

She flicked through the pages again, to see whether he had written this anywhere else. He hadn't. She pursed her lips, photographing the entry with her mobile phone, before sealing it in a fresh evidence bag.

In front of her, lying on his back, lay the body of Gethin Jenkins. The violence of his death was clear in the wide eyes, and gaping mouth, along with the blood-soaked pavement, his blood-soaked hands, and the spatter on the grass and the underside of the bridge. Arterial blood had had shot several feet, probably after he no longer had the strength to stem the flow with his hands.

Yvonne shuddered, looking both ways along the path, wondering from which direction the killer had come. She wondered why Gethin hadn't heard his attacker approach; the path was quiet. Had he been talking to someone on the phone? To her? To his killers?

"Dewi, can you call Callum and ask him to get hold of Gethin Jenkins' mobile phone records, as soon as possible. I want to know if he made any further calls after speaking to me. I would also like to know who he was regularly in contact with."

"On it."

∼

WHILST SOCO CONTINUED to work the crime scene, Yvonne, Dewi and Ian Rhys left them to it, heading to Jenkins' home in Llanwrtyd Wells.

The house, a two-bedroomed semi-detached property, contained little in the way of furniture.

"Definitely a man-pad." Yvonne muttered to her sergeant, eyeing the lack of clutter and dark mahogany furnishings.

"Oh, I don't know. I think this would be a bit too dark for me. And anyway, I knew a woman, once-"

"Okay. Okay." Yvonne held up her hand, breaking into a grin. "Fine. I didn't mean to be sexist. I'm sorry."

"I should think so, too." Dewi grinned back.

DC Rhys gave them fresh gloves. "Best not move anything until the photographer has been. He's on his way."

"I've got my body cam switched on." Dewi offered.

"Body cam's good." Rhys nodded.

Yvonne pursed her lips. "There's not much to show, for a life lived, is there?"

"No. I hope that means he spent time elsewhere, with loved ones, and not here on his own." DC Rhys sighed.

A quick look in the kitchen bin revealed a preponderance of ready-made meal boxes and packets, suggesting Gethin's social life was anything but lively.

Yvonne cast soulful eyes over the boxes, a lump in her throat and a gnawing in her gut.

"I guess this means the DCI won't pull us from the case now, eh?" Dewi began opening drawers.

"Well, we've got a full-blown murder investigation now, and if we have reason to link it to the mid-air collisions, I don't see how Llewelyn could take us off. Don't get excited, but I think it too much of a coincidence that someone murdered him when he was about to open up. I think they knew he would talk."

They continued going through his belongings for a further forty minutes, but found nothing to shed light on the note he had made. Who or what, the 'Hand of Darkness' was, was still a mystery.

Yvonne felt low as she walked back to the car with Dewi. She couldn't shake the feeling she was responsible for Gethin's death. She had, perhaps, placed him in an impossible position. Who knew Jenkins was about to talk?

13
DEEPER INTO THE MIRE

Royston Thomas opened the message and licked his lips. She knew just what to say.

Sweat beaded on his forehead and upper lip as he typed his reply. 'Can we meet? After all the things you've told me, I can't wait to meet you in person, get my hands on you.'

'Really? What would you do?'

Royston rubbed the back of his neck, thinking about it, shifting position in his chair as his state of arousal made him uncomfortable.

His wife's face appeared in his mind and he snapped the phone shut. He had never strayed. These conversations were heading in only one direction. He couldn't, could he?

He and Karen's sex life had reduced to a simmer. If he was honest, it was not even a simmer. Frenetic lives meant nighttime was for sleeping. Although they still talked, that conversation was rarely about their love life. Rather, it was about work, or the latest scrapes their friends had gotten into, or money, or whether-or-not they could afford a new kitchen. The minutiae of life. He couldn't remember the last time they had ripped each other's clothes off. And yet, with this woman he barely knew, this mysterious direct-message entity, he wanted to do exactly that, tear her clothes off and make love until they were both exhausted.

It was fantasy, and yet it felt more tangible than anything he had done in a long time.

"Royston, she's ready if you want to take her up." Tim Payne, slapped him on the back.

Royston stood, his lunch bag strategically placed in front of his groin. "Great, I'm good."

Tim handed him the keys. "Go easy. Monitor the weather. It's clear now, but there's a storm heading in later."

"Will do." Royston grabbed the keys, feeling his phone vibrating in his pocket. She had messaged again. He licked more sweat from his lip, but left his phone where it was. He would consider it later, when he had more time.

∼

YVONNE BLINKED several times under the bright lights of the mortuary and shifted the weight between her aching feet. Postmortems were never easy to watch, but the personal nature of this one heightened the nausea she felt.

They had washed the body clean of blood. Jenkins had soaked himself in it, in his desperate struggle to stem the flow. The remaining skin was ashen and mottled.

She swallowed, an uncomfortable lump in her throat. "I'm sorry," she wanted to say. "I'm sorry this happened to you. I hope I didn't catalyse this terrible event."

"Ready?" Hanson's voice forced her out of her reverie. She was grateful.

"I'm ready." She nodded, gagging as Hanson explored the wound. She kept her composure as best she could.

"It's a deep wound, made by a sharp knife. Just one cut, fast and accurate." Hanson grimaced. "The victim likely would not have known what was happening until it was too late. The wound goes to a depth of two inches, on the left side."

"Right-handed assailant?" Yvonne tilted her head to get a better look.

"I'd say, looking at the incision, the killer attacked him from behind. A right-handed attacker, cutting from left to right. The hands of the victim are unmarked, confirming my conclusion that he hadn't seen it coming. No defensive injuries of any kind."

Yvonne looked at her feet. "He had agreed to meet me that afternoon. He said he would tell me something important about a case and that he needed to do it face-to-face."

Hanson had either not heard her, or did not wish to comment. "From the blood at the scene, and on the victim's clothing, I would conclude that he had walked or stumbled a few feet prior to collapsing. He would not have been able to call out. His vocal cords were severed. It looks like he was trying to get help."

Yvonne could picture it all too vividly. Could see him stumbling along the river path, eyes wide; trying to summon help, noiseless save for the gurgling of his own blood as he tried to breathe through it.

She shuddered. "Anything else you can say about the perp, besides his being right-handed?"

Hanson pursed his lips. "Judging by the angle of the wound, I'd say the assailant was taller than his victim by two inches, at least. The killer angled the cutting edge upwards. I'll make accurate measurements and give you a more better height estimation in my report. It's for guidance only, obviously."

The DI nodded. "Weapon?"

"The wound is typical of a wide-bladed knife which tapers towards the end. I'd suggest a kitchen knife, specifically, a French cook's knife. They sharpened the blade for this attack. Whoever committed this offence, likely expected to use of this level of violence."

"So, unlikely to be a mugging-gone-wrong. More like a planned assassination?"

"I would say the evidence points to a planned murder, yes. They knew the victim would never leave the river path, alive."

"Thank you." Yvonne took a last look at the body of the man with whom she had so recently felt confounded. Little had she known what his fate would be, but she was more determined than ever to get to the bottom of whatever was going on.

14

SOMETHING AND NOTHING

"What do we have on the pilots of the Clywedog dam collision?" Yvonne asked, after she had briefed the team about Gethin's postmortem.

"We've spoken to Mrs Sharon Tranchard, Kevin Tranchard's wife." Callum checked his notes. "She's distraught, as you might imagine. He left her and their three children behind. Two boys aged eleven and five years, and a little girl, aged three."

The DI sighed. "Those poor kids. Did you ask her how he was, prior to the incident?"

"We did, ma'am. She states, her husband was physically and mentally well. When pressed, she admitted to his having been a little quieter than usual in the month before his death."

"What did she mean by quiet?"

"Not as talkative. Deep in thought. She said she suspected that it was employment-related. He worked for the Forestry Commission, and had been drawing up plans for planting a swathe of new land, in the government's push to combat climate change. Apparently, he'd been in talks with farmers, about adapting their land. Those talks had not gone well."

"Any visits to his doctor?"

"None. His wife stated he hadn't visited his GP in two years, not since an injury to his wrist."

"I see. Any previous incidents, as regards his piloting?"

Callum shook his head. "No previous accidents, according to his wife. Airport records corroborate this. Apparently, he was a stickler for rules and would not have skimped or cut corners on his pre-flight checks."

"What about the other pilot? Tom Yates?"

"Not married and no children. He has, however, left behind his partner Chloe Yates. They'd been together just shy of five years. Again, according to Chloe, Tom had no physical or mental issues. She admitted to them having had regular arguments, however, and they came close to splitting up last summer. She said they worked through their problems, and states they there was no argument on the day of the collision, nor on the day before. Yates was not taking prescription drugs and consumed alcohol rarely. She states she had never known him to use illicit drugs."

"So, nothing in the histories of either pilot, that would explain what happened. What have the AAIB said?"

"They've sent the wreckage to Farnborough, for their engineers to check the planes, but they believe there was nothing mechanically wrong with them. They are all in shock after losing a colleague, but they don't appear to suspect any link between Gethin Jenkins' death and the mid-air collisions."

Yvonne nodded. "I see. Well, they might be right, though I don't think so. I think there is a link, and we may be the only ones looking for it."

"They said an engineering inspector is likely to join us

next week. However, because of the distance he has to travel, he won't be staying, and is likely to make only one or two visits, altogether. They expect the investigation will only take two months, three at the outside."

The DI sighed. "Well, the DCI hasn't pulled us from the collisions investigation, yet. So, in the meantime, we continue what we're doing and digging up everything we can around those pilots' lives. Dai, I'd like you to monitor Michaela Harris and Ryan Aston. I think they are having an affair, and she stands to benefit form a substantial insurance payout on Philip Nugent's death. Could be something or nothing, but if they're having a relationship, we should look at them more closely. Questions?"

Dai tapped his pen on his chin. "Did we get anything back from Farnborough regarding the memory sticks from Keith Files' simulator?"

"Good question, Dai. I don't know. Could you contact them today and enquire?"

"Will do."

∽

ALTHOUGH IT HAD BEEN a long day, Yvonne whooped at the holdall dumped in the hallway. Tasha was home from London.

She ran to the lounge; tiredness lifting as she saw her partner sipping a glass of white, one eye on the television, and the other on the papers on her lap.

"Yvonne." Tasha moved the papers onto the coffee table and rose to give the DI a hug. "Am I glad to see you. I've missed you. It seems ages."

Yvonne hugged her back. "I'm excited to see you, too."

Neither noticed the wine spilling from the psychologist's glass.

"I thought I would surprise you." Tasha gave her a wine-flavoured kiss. "I've got a lasagne cooking in the oven."

Yvonne's smile lit her face. She appeared years younger. "Great. I'll grab a glass of wine, lay the table, and have a quick shower. It's been a helluva day and a mad week, altogether. I am so thrilled to see you."

∽

Despite its being delicious, Yvonne found herself unable to eat much of the meal.

"Are you all right?" Tasha asked, tilting her head, and placing a hand over Yvonne's. "Do you want to talk about it?"

The DI wiped a tear from her eye.

"Yvonne?" Tasha frowned.

"A colleague was murdered a few days ago."

"Oh god, I am so sorry. Who? Not Dewi?"

"No, it wasn't a police colleague. It's no-one you would know. He was a colleague from the Air Accident Investigation Bureau. A Human Factors inspector, sent to investigate the Welshpool mid-air collision."

"I see." Tasha's hand remained on Yvonne's. "What happened?"

The DI related the circumstances of his death.

"Oh, God, that's awful. Are you linking his murder to the air crashes?"

The DI nodded, a rogue tear wending its way down her cheek. "I am. I thought he knew something more about the collisions than he was telling us. I suspected him of brushing things under the carpet, and I'd been trying to work out what was going on with him."

"Did you suspect him of being involved?"

"I thought he was being bribed or blackmailed."

"Surely, not?"

"I don't know." Yvonne shook her head. "Aspects of his behaviour were not adding up for me. I had relatives telling me one thing, while he was telling me another. I was hard on him as a result, Tasha."

"I can see how upset you are." Tasha got up to hold her. "It must have come as a terrible shock."

The DI's eyes glistened with the tears she was holding back. "I threatened him. I told him that I suspected him of wrong-doing and, if he didn't come clean with me, I would expose him."

"You think they killed him because of what he knew? Because of something he was helping to cover up?"

"I called him on the morning he died. He told me he wanted to meet me in the afternoon. Said he had something to tell me, but was only willing to do so in person. We would have met at the Bank Tearooms, but..." The DI let out a sob.

"Come here." Tasha took hold of her and rocked her gently. "Don't blame yourself. Whatever he had gotten himself into, it was his responsibility, not yours. If involved in some sort of racket, he would have known who he was getting into bed with, and would have known of the risks well enough. You didn't get him into it, and you have a job to do. A very important job which he should have been helping you with, not hindering the investigation." Tasha's tone softened. "What happened to him, anyway?"

"Didn't you see the news?"

"No. I've been neck-deep in the Met case. I'd just switched on the television, when you got home."

"He had his throat slit, under Builth bridge."

"Oh, God." Tasha gaped. "No-one deserves that."

"No, and I can't help but suspect a link between his death and my case. I really felt like he was hiding or destroying evidence. I thought he had wiped memory sticks belonging to a pilot involved in the Welshpool crash. The data would have been from a flight simulator. I had been wondering if that pilot had been practising flying into other aircraft."

Tasha leaned back. "Really?"

Yvonne sighed, shaking her head. "I don't know. It was an idea. I really don't know what might have been on those sticks. I didn't see them for myself, and they are now at labs in Farnborough. Or, at least, that is what Jenkins told me he had done with them. There was something about the way he told me... it just..."

"Have you contacted Farnborough to ask about them?"

"No. The DCI wanted to pull us from the case. I didn't want Farnborough reminding Llewelyn that it's time for us to go."

"Well, I think you should inform the DCI. I am always amazed by your intuition." Tasha smiled. "If you suspect it, then it's definitely worth chasing it up. Now, eat that lasagne."

15

TAKEN OFF THE CASE

"Yvonne, can I have a word?"

She turned to face Llewelyn, who walked away from her, heading towards his office.

Raising her eyebrows at Dewi, she ran down the corridor after him.

"Sir?" She closed his office door behind her, catching her breath.

"How are you coping, after the terrible business with Jenkins?" He ran his hand through his hair. "How is everyone bearing up?"

"We're okay. It's made us even more determined to get to the bottom of the air collisions."

He nodded. "I wanted to speak to you about that."

"Really?"

"Well, I still see no reason for us to continue investigating the collisions. I think it's appropriate to aid in the investigation into Gethin's murder, that's within our jurisdiction, but the AAIB can deal the air accidents. They have the budget and the knowhow. We can provide information and support where needed, but let them do the legwork. It's what they are there for."

"But, sir, I can't help feeling that Jenkins' murder links in with these bizarre air crashes, somehow. Gethin wanted to talk to me about it face-to-face. Why was that? I think someone assassinated him."

Llewelyn held up his hand. "That's melodramatic, isn't it? You know there have been two previous muggings in the Builth area in the last six months. An elderly gentleman, left lying in a ditch at the Builth show, and a lady, knocked over in a bag-snatch in the town centre in the first week of October. Llandod CID have been working that case. They think it likely, Gethin's murder resulted from an attempted mugging, especially since his phone and wallet were missing."

"Yes, but those other muggings did not result in anyone's murder. I mean, why kill Jenkins and not the first two victims? There was no mention of knives in the other muggings, was there?"

"Escalation? Jenkins resisted?"

"He had no defensive wounds. Hanson is adamant, they took Jenkins unawares. He had no time to react."

"They have CCTV footage of a hooded youth on the river path. Useless for facial identification, but there are similarities with the hooded man caught on CCTV during the town centre bag snatch."

"Can I see it?"

"See what?"

"The CCTV footage for both incidents, if you have it."

Llewelyn sighed. "I don't have it, I'm afraid."

"Then what makes you so sure the two figures are similar?"

"Well, I thought that would be obvious? Our CID

colleagues in Llandod told me. You can read the email, if you like."

She shook her head. "It's okay, I'll contact them and ask them to email me copies of everything. I need to see it for myself."

"Very well. I still want you to wind down your team's involvement in the air crash investigations."

Yvonne bit her lip. "Is that all, sir?"

He nodded. "For now."

∽

Yvonne huffed as she rejoined her DS. "That man can be exasperating."

"What's he said?" Dewi handed her a fresh brew.

"He's still insisting we pull out of further investigation of the crashes."

"What about what happened to Jenkins?"

"He's okay with us providing information to the murder investigation because Gethin was working in our area, but Llandod CID have it that his death was a mugging-gone-wrong, and the DCI is happy to run with that. I bet the commissioner has been on his back about spending." Yvonne threw her pen down on the desk. "I'm requesting copies of all the CCTV footage they have. I'll be the first to apologise if I have this all wrong, but I think Jenkins' death is a coincidence too far."

∽

Royston Thomas finished his dinner, his gaze travelling to his wife's downcast expression. "Are you okay, love?"

Karen placed her knife and fork down, and pushed her plate away, shaking her head. "Not really."

"Want to talk about it?"

She sighed. "Where are we going, Royston? Or, where are we going wrong?"

He felt hot blood spreading through his cheeks. "What makes you think we are going wrong, love?"

"You seem distant from me, these days. Sometimes, I feel like I hardly know you."

He pushed back his chair, rising to grab hold of her hand. "Let's talk about it."

He led her from the dining room, to the fire in the lounge as it crackled in the hearth.

Sitting next to her on the sofa, he turned her to face him, holding her shoulders. "I'm sorry, if I've seemed distant. It's not you, or us, it's the-"

His phone buzzed in his pocket.

He ignored it. "I've been crazy-busy at work, and at the hangar. It's been one of those-"

His phone buzzed again.

"Aren't you going to get that?" Karen narrowed her eyes.

He shook his head. "It won't be a call. It's likely another message from Tim. They've stepped up the amount of pre-flight checking we have to do. The investigators are going through everything with a fine-tooth comb."

His phone buzzed once more. The muscles in his face flickered, his clenched knuckles pale against his jeans. "I'll turn it off."

He pulled the phone from his front pocket and pushed the side button off, without checking who the message was from. He knew full well who it was.

Doing his best to reassure Karen, he poured her a glass of wine, and himself an ale.

Once she had settled in front of the television, he moved to the garage at the side of the house and switched his phone back on.

There were several messages from her.

'Hi.'

'Hello?'

'Where are you?'

'Why aren't you answering?'

His felt sick, the blood rushed to his face, causing the veins in his temples to protrude.

He sent a reply, 'Leave me alone. I can't do this anymore. I don't want to message you, and I don't want to meet you.'

'You didn't say that yesterday.'

'What?'

'When you met me for sex.'

'What? What are you talking about?'

'Oh, I see. Like that, is it? You'r gunna pretend nothing happened, because I'm underage.'

'What? Leave me alone. You're not right. You need help.'

'You didn't say that yesterday, neither. You were mad keen on me being underage, then.'

Royston wiped his hand across his damp forehead. Conscious, too, of the wet in his armpits and down his spine. He shook his head, turning his phone off. He ran into the garden and vomited into the hedge.

16

STAKEOUT

"Think we're on a fool's errand?" Dai passed the pack of digestives to Callum.

"Don't know."

"I'm not sure I agree with Yvonne on this. She's got a bee in her bonnet but, if you look at it objectively, what exactly have we got to go on? Second day of surveillance, and Michaela Harris has not even left the house. And Ryan Aston hasn't come near the place. Meanwhile, we're sat here like two lemons. I mean, it's not even as though we have proof of any crime, is it? What exactly are we investigating? It's like giving children busy-work to keep them out of mischief. That's what this is."

"Shh." Callum gripped the steering wheel.

"Well-"

"Shh. There's a car pulling up. Looks like a black Audi. It's several hundred metres behind us. Let's see who gets out."

Dai glanced in his side mirror. "Okay, watching. Can't see anyone, yet."

"Someone's getting out." Callum sank down in his seat,

eyes up at his rear-view mirror. "It's him. It's Aston. Keep low. All we need is evidence he's seeing her. Very suspicious, that he parks his car so far away, when there's a space right outside her house."

"He's still walking this way," Dai agreed. "Dirty dog."

"Well, we don't know they are up to something but, since he told us his last visit was a one-off, after trying to deny it altogether, I'd say he's in her knickers. Wouldn't you?"

They watched in silence, as Ryan Aston walked the rest of the way to Michaela Harris's door.

"Bingo." Callum whistled. "And we have it on dash cam. Get out of this one, Aston."

"Let's see how long he's in there for. Damn, I wish we had coffee to dunk these biscuits."

∽

ROYSTON PUT his rucksack inside the hangar and crossed to where Tim Payne was working on a Cessna, with his son Rob standing by.

"Tim. Rob." Royston greeted each of them with a nod.

"Royston." Tim stopped tinkering and wiped his hands on a rag he pulled from the front pocket of his overalls. "You're late, man. Where've you been?"

Royston shrugged, aware he was being analysed. "I've been busy at work, you know. There's something I wanted to talk to you about." He drew himself up to his full height, jutting his chin. "Not now, though."

"Good, well, give me a hand with these bolts, will you?" Tim handed him a spanner.

∽

THE ENGINE FIRED up the first time. "She's sounding good, isn't she?" Tim grinned. "Job well done, I'd say."

"Listen, Tim. I need to talk to you."

"Fire away." Tim answered, wiping more grease from his hands.

Royston flicked his head toward Rob Payne. "I'd rather speak in private, if possible."

"Rob?" Tim placed a hand on his son's arm. "Fancy popping to the garage and getting us some sandwiches?"

Rob pulled a face. "Do I have to?"

Tim tilted his head. "We haven't eaten, yet. I could do with some food. It'll only take five minutes, son."

Rob kicked at the dust on the concrete floor. "Fine, I'll go."

Royston watched until Rob had disappeared out of the hangar, the latter tapping his phone as he disappeared.

"Well? What is it?" Tim approached Royston. "What's going on, mate?"

Royston sighed. "I've got myself into a bit of bother." He wiped his hand across his brow. "I'm scared of Karen finding out. I don't want to hurt her."

Royston's phone chimed at full volume in his pocket. "Oh, hell."

He pulled it out, punching the green symbol. "What?"

Royston paled as he listened to the caller. His hand trembled as he replaced the phone. "Look, Tim, I've got to go. I'll... I'll catch up with you another time."

"Royston?"

"I've got to go." Royston grabbed his bag and fled the hangar, leaving Tim Payne scratching his head, deep lines creasing the latter's forehead.

17

FLASHBACK

"Good work." Yvonne stood, hands on hips. "So, Ryan Aston was in with her for three-and-a-half hours."

"That's right." Callum nodded. "He squeezed her arm, and pecked her cheek, as he left."

"Well, that's not proof of very much on its own. However, given that he denied knowing her very well, and that his visit to her last time was a one-off, I'd say this is indicative that something else is going on. Did you get anything from social media?"

Callum shook his head. "There's no evidence that we could find. They are being careful in that regard. They have their friend lists hidden. We'd need a warrant to get access to their direct messages."

"Yes. Have we had the printouts from Gethin's phone company, yet?"

"We have, ma'am. Beside yourself, there was one other number on the record. It was a call shortly after yours."

"We're working on the source of that call, but the

number was a pay-as-you-go mobile, and the phone was purchased in a supermarket in Newtown. The details given by the purchaser were false. The address doesn't exist. The street does, but the number doesn't."

"Oh, why am I not surprised? Have the supermarket got CCTV of the purchaser?"

"No, ma'am. The system has already recorded over any footage they might have had. They only keep footage for a day or two before the system records over it."

Yvonne sighed. "Two steps forward, three steps back. This case is a mess."

～

Yvonne ambled to her car, her mind full airfields and mangled metal.

Not for the first time that day, she pondered another airfield many miles away. A glider in pieces on smashed cars. A ruptured fuel tank bursting into black smoke and orange flame.

A sickening dread welled within her, and she was back there, at Sherbourne, her husband trapped inside a glider's wreckage.

Though years had passed, images were as vivid as they ever were. Like a wormhole opening in the brain, allowing events to travel so perfectly through time, she could still smell them. Touch them. Taste them. Like it was the first time.

Although the years had done their bit to ease the horrible rawness of it, pain still lived in the remembrance.

She considered the pilots of the latest crashes, and the anguish felt by the families of the dead. Twelve men, grieved for by a myriad friends and family. Her heart went out to them all, victims and loved ones alike. None would be the same again.

18

SINISTER

A red-faced Royston stared at his phone, nostrils flared. 'What do you want?'

'To talk.'

'Why won't you stop and leave me alone.'

'I'll talk to your wife.'

'And tell her what? I have done nothing.'

'My friends will support everything I tell her. Karen. That's her name, right?'

'Leave my wife out of this. Leave her alone.'

'Then do as we ask.'

'Which is what?'

'Meet us at the roundabout at Coed-y-Dinas at 9 am, tomorrow.'

'And if I don't?'

'You better make sure you come alone.'

∽

He parked in the car park at the shopping centre, glancing around for the would-be contacts.

The place was half-full already.

He stuffed his hands into his pockets and walked to the roundabout, clouds of breath curling around his face.

Like something from a gang movie, three figures in hooded coats stood at the roundabout. Their faces indiscernible, because of the scarves they had tied around their mouths beneath their hoods. Their eyes were in shadow.

He got the impression, from their body shapes, that two were male and one female.

"Give us your phone." A male ordered, his voice deep and gruff.

"No," Royston countered.

The same male opened up his jacket to show a knife blade glinting from a home-made, inside pocket.

Sweat beaded on Royston's forehead.

The male held his hand to the knife.

"All right. All right." Royston took out his phone and looked at it, frowning. He extended his hand in slow motion, not daring to take his eyes off the male with the knife.

They snatched the phone from him. "You'll get this back when you've done what we ask."

"Which is what?" Royston took a step back. "What do you want from me?"

"We want you to do a little favour for us."

"What sort of favour?" Sweat pooled at the base of the pilot's spine.

"We want you to fly at another plane and miss by inches."

"What?"

"You heard. You got to fly your plane at someone else and miss them by inches."

"Why?"

"Because we want you to."

Royston shook his head. "No way, that's madness. I won't do it, and there is no way you can make me. I'm going to the police."

The menacing male took a step forward, opening his jacket to show the knife again. "That would be a stupid thing to do."

"I would lose either my life or my licence." Royston gritted his teeth, tempted to deck the male, despite the knife.

"We'll destroy your life if you don't do what we ask. One near miss. That's it. Do it good. Make it look like an accident, and you'll get to keep your licence and your wife."

"When?"

"We'll let you know."

"I could be killed. I could kill someone else."

The male shrugged. "Better make sure you get it right, then."

A black car pulled up on the road. Royston could only see the very top.

The three figures ran for it.

The pilot was sure one of them was a female. Probably, the female he had been messaging. All wore ill-fitting clothing. He retched, desperately thinking of a way out. He made his way back to the car, the weight of conscience constricting his chest like a tourniquet.

19

A KILLER LURKS

Michaela Harris waited in reception.
Yvonne studied her on the monitor for two minutes.

The woman paced the floor, running her hands through her hair, constantly checking her watch.

Each time someone entered reception, Michaela swung round, eyes wide, hand to her chest.

Dewi joined the DI. "Ready?"

Yvonne nodded. "She's worried about something, Dewi. Let's see what she has to say."

"Would you like to come with us, Miss Harris?" Yvonne asked, pushing open the door to the corridor.

Michaela nodded, signaling acquiescence, but the DI sensed her interviewee wanted to run in the other direction.

"Do you prefer Miss Harris or Michaela?" Yvonne asked, when they entered the interview room.

"Michaela," she said, the name rattling through a clogged throat. She made several attempts and finally cleared the blockage.

"Michaela, you should know that there is a camera in

the corner above you." Yvonne pointed to it. "It will record all of our conversation. I understand you brought no one with you. Would you like to call anyone to support you? We have a duty solicitor, if you would like one."

"Why?" Michaela's eyes darted from Yvonne, to Dewi, and back. "Am I under arrest? Have I done something wrong?"

"No, you are not under arrest. We only wish to talk to you about Philip, and your relationship with him. I suggested someone accompany you, because it might help you feel more comfortable and you would have advice if you need it. If we think you need legal counsel, at any point, we will stop the interview in order for you to have a solicitor. Is that okay? Equally, you may ask for counsel at any point."

Michaela nodded, wiping her hands on her jeans and straightening her jumper.

"How have you been? I realise this time must have been difficult for you."

"I've been on a roller coaster." Michaela's mouth turned down. "I haven't been sleeping well. I miss him."

Yvonne nodded, her eyes softened. "It's devastating, losing a partner. Were you aware he took out an insurance policy, with a substantial pay-out, six weeks before his death? Did he tell you about it?"

Michaela eyed the DI as though she was ruminating something. "Of course. I've instructed a solicitor to look into it."

"Did Philip warn you he would take out insurance?"

Michaela nodded, examining her fingernails.

"Is that a yes?"

"Yes."

"What were your thoughts?"

"I don't know."

"Did you ask him why he was taking out the policy?"

Michaela shook her head.

"Were you not curious about it?"

"Not really. It was insurance. A safety net. I never thought we would actually need it."

"Was he doing it for the baby?"

"Probably."

"Did he give you any reason to suspect he might be suicidal?"

"No."

"Were you aware he was taking anti-depressants again?"

Michaela shifted in her seat. "No."

"We confirmed with his doctor that he had visited the surgery five months prior to his death. This would have been when you noticed he had renewed his prescription. You stated that he renewed it merely as a precaution. However, the doctor had given a fresh diagnosis of depression. Did Philip not mention this to you?"

"He'd get moody sometimes, but I didn't think he was ill again. I thought he was okay, maybe a little tired. Unless…"

"Unless?"

"Unless he was hiding it from me… because of the pregnancy."

"What were his thoughts about the baby?"

Michaela's eyes darted to the DI's face. "What do you mean?"

"I mean, was he happy about the pregnancy or did he have concerns about it?"

The girl shook her head. "I thought he was happy."

"I only ask, because his visit to the GP would have been around the time you became pregnant."

"I don't think it would have been about the baby. My pregnancy was the one thing he got excited about."

Yvonne nodded. "Okay."

"Can I go now?" Michaela sighed.

"Just one or two more questions, if that is all right?" The DI looked at her notes. "How do you know Ryan Aston?"

"What?"

"How long have you known him?"

Michaela coloured. "He's a friend. I've only known him for two months." She shrugged.

"Really?" Yvonne straightened in her chair. "So, you knew him prior to Philip's death?"

Yvonne shot a glance at her DS.

"Yes."

"But, only for two months, or so?"

"That's right."

"Well, that's interesting. Mr Aston told us that he didn't know you prior to Philip's death, and that he only visited you, as a one-off, on the day we came to see you. Why would he do that? We passed him as we were leaving your house. He was coming as we were going."

Michaela covered her mouth with her hand. "Well, maybe that's right. I've just lost my partner. I get confused."

"We think you knew Ryan Aston prior to your partner's death, and that you were having an affair with him. That you have known him for over two months."

"I-"

"We're not here to judge you, Miss Harris, we're just exploring Philip's mental state, and his motivations."

"You think that my having an affair with Ryan was a reason for Philip to kill himself? Is that it?" Michaela pulled a face, tears welling in her eyes. "I don't care what you say. I don't believe Philip was suicidal. I would have known."

"And you don't know why he might have taken out such a large insurance policy?"

Michaela stood up. "I want to go. Unless you are charging me with a crime, I am free to go. Am I right?"

"Absolutely. We didn't mean to upset you." Yvonne sighed. "We wouldn't be doing our job, or justice to Mr Nugent, if we didn't fully investigate the circumstances around his death. That sometimes means asking difficult questions of those who loved him. We try not to leave any stone unturned. You can surely understand that?"

Michaela paused. "You're right. I was seeing Ryan Aston. Maybe Philip found out, and I didn't realise. I will have to live with that thought for the rest of my life. I still don't believe he was suicidal, and I was the closest person to him. I should know. Can I go now?"

Yvonne stood. "Just to be clear, we have no reason to blame you for your partner's death. You are free to go. Thank you for coming in to see us today."

∽

"What do you make of that?" Dewi tutted. "She was very jumpy about Aston and the insurance."

Yvonne nodded, pursing her lips. "She's been having an affair and has probably already beaten herself up about it since Philip's death. She doesn't look happy. She's human. People have affairs. It happens. I don't believe she had anything to do with her partner's death, and we don't know that he was responsible for Files' plane smashing into the other aircraft. However, I would like to speak to Ryan Aston again."

∽

YVONNE GATHERED the team round to watch the CCTV footage they had received from Llandrindod Wells CID.

"Come on, come on," she muttered as they chatted amongst themselves, waiting for the kettle to boil for their brew, grabbing pencils and pens. "Some time today would be good" She tapped her pen on the desk.

She cleared her throat as the noise died down. "Just to remind you all, the two clips you are about to see are from a bag snatch in Builth town centre and footage from the river path, before and after the murder of Gethin Jenkins. The bag snatch happened three weeks prior to Gethin Jenkins' death. Look carefully. Could they be the same person? Or, are we looking at two different perpetrators? Llandrindod CID are hedging their bets but, on balance, they feel it likely it is the same offender on both occasions. If it is the same person, then, perhaps, Gethin's murder was a mugging gone wrong. But, if these are two different perpetrators, we continue to investigate his death as possibly linked to the air collisions we have been seeing in Powys."

No-one spoke as she pressed play.

The first clip showed a middle-aged woman in a yellow mac, walking along the high street, approached from behind by a figure in dark clothing.

After the clip, the DI summarised what they had witnessed. "The snatch took microseconds; the offender slipping her bag off her right arm and running with it. The victim didn't realise what had happened until he had gotten several paces, and she tripped as she tried to run after him."

"Okay, now for clip two, on the river path. We see the suspect before he goes under the bridge. Watch his gait. He disappears, and will reappear within twenty seconds, going back the way he came. Unfortunately, we lose him after that, as the camera further along the path was not operational because of a technical fault."

Yvonne played each clip twice more, hoping they were seeing what she was, the person in the second clip was a heavier build and had more of a swagger to his walk. The clothing was similar, but too indistinct to help in terms of comparison. "Well, what do you think?"

"Two different people." Dewi nodded for emphasis. "I'm sure of it. I would even go so far, as to say, I think there is a gender difference. The bag snatcher looked female, to me."

"Interesting." Yvonne looked around the rest of the faces.

"I agree, two different offenders," Callum concurred.

Dai was not as certain as his colleagues. He shook his head. "The CCTV is not clear enough, for me. I can't say whether they are the same or different."

Yvonne nodded. "Thanks for your honesty, Dai. My feeling is that these are two different people, and I agree with Dewi, that the bag snatcher was possibly female."

"So, where does that leave us?" Dai sipped his tea.

"I can take our thoughts to the DCI, to support our continued involvement in investigating both Gethin's death, and the air collisions, because of their possibly being linked. I don't think we can close that line of enquiry, yet. As we have a majority agreement, I will go back to the DCI."

Callum shook his head. "I can't believe the murder was over so quickly. The killer was in and out."

Yvonne sighed. "I know, it's frightening how fast we can take a life. Like Hanson said, Jenkins didn't see it coming."

∼

KAREN LOOKED across at her husband. He'd barely touched his dinner. "Didn't you like it?"

"Like what?" Royston turned to her with glazed eyes.

"Your dinner. You know, the one going cold in front of you. That dinner."

"Oh." Royston picked up his knife and fork.

"Where were you?" She asked, head tilted; her expression gentle.

"I was thinking about my next flight." He shrugged. He was telling the truth. He had thought of little else except his next flight, since the sinister meeting at Coed-y-Dinas.

"I could make you something else?" Karen suggested, he still not having tried even a mouthful.

"No, I'm sorry." He took a forkful of pasta and smiled at her. "You know I love you, don't you?"

"Of course." Her eyes twinkled as her husband reached over to hold her hand in his.

His thoughts turned to the girl. She had destroyed their conversations on social media. He cursed himself for not having saved them somewhere. It had been the only evidence to support his version that there had been no impropriety, and definitely no mention of her being underage, until she sprang that on him. He still didn't know whether he believed that she was that young.

He looked at his wife's concerned face and knew he could not go to the police. He couldn't bear the thought of Karen finding out. It would devastate her. She would probably leave. He couldn't let that happen. But that left him with a ridiculous and risky daredevil stunt to complete, or risk losing everything. Who were these people, and why were they so evil? How had he ever allowed himself to become entangled with them?

20

FARNBOROUGH

Yvonne perused the information they had received from Farnborough and the interim report on the Welshpool collision.

"What are they saying?" Dewi asked, peering over her shoulder.

She leaned back in her chair, chewing on a pen lid. "They've found no mechanical fault with either plane. At least, none that would explain what happened. They say their final report is likely to conclude the crash occurred due to pilot error."

"Really?" Dewi perched on the edge of her desk.

"Apparently, Gethin emailed them to say he had found nothing to support the hypothesis of pilot suicide, and pilot error is all that remains, when they have ruled out all other possibilities. So, that is that, as far as the AAIB is concerned. And, how can we argue it? They can wash their hands of the Welshpool crash. It will be merely another statistic."

"Well, to be fair, they have a point. What have we got? I mean, what have we really got, to even suggest that a crime has taken place? If only you had had that conversation with Gethin."

Yvonne whirled her chair around to face him. "We have a dead AAIB inspector. No, we have a murdered AAIB inspector, who was hiding or destroying evidence, prior to his death. One who, when I challenged him, wanted to meet me in secret to discuss what he was up to. Our killers slaughtered him, before he got the chance. I agree, it wouldn't hold up in court, but for heaven's sake." She sighed. "There's much more to this, I know there is."

Dewi nodded. "I wish we had found his wallet and phone."

"Well, we know the phone was destroyed soon after they killed him. The wallet? Probably emptied and tossed into the river."

"I wonder how they are getting on with the wreckage from the Clywedog crash?" Dewi walked to the window, peering out at the overcast sky.

"Well, if I was a betting woman, I'd put money on there being no mechanical fault there, either. What I want to know, is who, or what, is the Hand of Darkness. Sounds like a gang or a terrorist organisation. Dig into it, will you, Dewi? See what you can find."

"Will do, ma'am."

~

She appreciated the silence as she drove to Clywedog still in awe of the rich, autumnal colours decorating her route. The trees were in their final bloom, displaying their deepest colours of plum, orange and gold. Half the leaves had flown already. The other half would join them soon enough.

Winter-proper would bed in, wrapping its hoary tendrils around all, whitening the landscape. Leaving it threadbare.

It was the weekend. She was working on her own time, since Tasha hadn't made it back. She felt her partner's absence in the pit of her stomach. Getting out and about was her way of dealing with it.

She couldn't shake the feeling that the crashes were someone's entertainment. After all, if someone was behind this, they had to be getting something from it. The team had examined all avenues around share-price fraud and found nothing.

Though keeping an open mind about insurance scamming by Michaela Harris and her current, or her late partner, she felt that scenario unlikely. Michaela and Ryan Aston would not set up other crashes to hide their scam behind, surely?

She parked in a lay-by next to a picnic bench with a panoramic view over the dam. Like the best oil painting, it lay calm and tranquil, the senescent leaves of the surrounding foliage, throwing up golds, russets and reds, to rival the best sunset.

Her breath lingered in ephemeral clouds, like those peppering the azure sky above her. She stared at it, seeing two planes in her mind's eye, approaching across the dam. No matter which way she looked, visibility could not have been the issue. To her mind, there was no way those planes did not see each other.

So why collide? What had gone wrong out there? Not for the first time, she wished the young couple had watched the first plane for a little longer. Not that she wished upon them the trauma of witnessing of an air disaster, but at least they would have more of an idea of what happened, without waiting for scraps from Farnborough.

Yvonne sat at the bench, breaking out her sandwiches of homemade tuna and cucumber, while continuing to contemplate the accident.

A group of males and a female approached, she estimated they were late-teens to early-twenties. They gathered a few hundred yards away from her, laughing and bantering. The males were taking turns pushing each other into the foliage.

Her thoughts turned to Tasha. She hoped the psychologist was all right, and making headway with the Met case, more headway than Yvonne and her team, at least.

21

CLUTCHING AT STRAWS

She rapped the DCI's door and took a deep breath, smoothing her skirt and straightening her hair.

"Come in." The DCI was in full uniform, tie straight; the buttons and stars on his tunic, reflected the overhead lighting. "Ah, Yvonne. Take a seat. What can I do for you?"

She couldn't help returning his smile. His eyes gleamed like the buttons on his jacket.

"I want more time to investigate the air collisions, sir."

He shook his head. "Wrap it up. I said tomorrow, didn't I?"

"You look very smart, sir."

"What? Er..., thank you." He shook his head. "We've got a big meeting today. The area is getting an extra forty-two uniformed officers. We've got to bang our heads together, to decide where to best deploy them. I'll be helping the crime commissioner, and the chief super, make the case for some of them coming to the Newtown area, given our ongoing nightmare with County Lines drug issues. Keep your fingers crossed for us, will you?"

She nodded. "I will, sir, of course." She remained standing. "About the air collisions? Could you give us an extra two or three weeks on it?"

Llewelyn sighed. "Yvonne, there really isn't the need. The AAIB have gathered all the evidence. We have their interim report into the Welshpool crash. And, as you very well know, they believe it was pilot error. We don't have an endless budget. We can't continue to throw money at this."

"But-"

"Besides," he continued. "It's protocol, for us to step back when no criminal intent comes to light. You know it is."

"But, what about the murder of Gethin Jenkins?"

"What about it? God rest his soul. He was in the wrong place at the wrong time. Llandod are more than capable of handling the investigation, and they've linked it to string of other muggings."

"What if they're wrong?" Yvonne's pupils widened, rendering her eyes charcoal black.

"So, let me get this straight." Llewelyn sighed. "Farnborough are wrong and Llandod CID are wrong. That's what you're telling me."

Her stance relaxed, as she placed her hands either side of her head. "Look, I know I may come across as some kind of crazy, but I talked to the witnesses of the Welshpool and Brecon crashes. Something is off. Keith Files wanted to crash his plane into the other plane. Why? He had no connection to the other pilot."

"The AAIB concluded pilot error. They had the evidence."

"Yes, but they did not have all the evidence, I am convinced that Gethin Jenkins destroyed some of it. I don't know why, but I know that he wanted to talk to me about it. To explain. He told me he needed to do that in person.

Someone got to him. Someone took him out. The question is, who, and why?"

"Yvonne, listen to what you are saying."

"Look, I know it sounds far-fetched, but his body language, his eye contact, everything screamed at me, he was covering up. Either that, or downright lying about the memory sticks he found at Files' house. When I threatened to expose him, he got very agitated. It was after that, he contacted me and asked me to meet him."

"Wouldn't you have been agitated, if a colleague had accused you of covering up evidence? Of not doing your job properly?"

"Look, all I know is he arranged to meet me and was murdered before he could."

"Right." The DCI sighed.

"The phone company confirmed he made another call, after the one with myself. The number was for a pay-as-you-go phone and we have not traced the owner. I believe whoever called him is the same person who had him killed. Further, I think he was probably being watched to make sure he didn't spill. They had something on him. I think he was being blackmailed and made to destroy evidence."

"You say, 'they', like you think it is a group or network. I have a lot of respect for you as my DI, but Christ, Yvonne, you're beginning to sound like a conspiracy theorist. What you are giving me is conjecture, and not evidence. You can't convict on gut feelings."

She sighed, rubbing her eyes. "I know. One last thing, if you'll hear me out. Gethin had written 'The Hand of Darkness' in his notebook and underlined it three times, like it was important. He wrote it next to his notes on the Brecon crash. If we are dealing with an organisation, that could be the name they have given themselves."

"Hand of Darkness?" Llewelyn pulled a face. "Sounds like the title of a book, or a movie, perhaps? What's on at Builth cinema?"

Yvonne glowered at him. "Can I have an extra two weeks, or not? For what it's worth, myself and my team scrutinised the CCTV footage from Builth and felt that the perpetrator of the town centre bag snatch, and the suspect captured on the river path before and after Jenkins' murder, are not the same person." She paused for breath, feeling drained.

Llewelyn pursed his lips. "Two weeks, you say? Hmm, let me think about it. I'll give you my answer tomorrow morning. Give me a file containing copies of everything you have got, including witness statements. It'll be my bedtime reading."

She sighed. "Thank you, sir."

∽

RYAN ASTON LICKED the sweat from his upper lip as he entered the interview room.

Yvonne explained the procedure. "You refused counsel," she reminded him. "Is that still your wish?"

"I don't need a solicitor. I have done nothing wrong." Aston gave her strong eye contact.

"Tell me about your relationship with Michaela."

"Relationship? What relationship would that be?"

The DI sighed, swapping glances with Callum. "Mr Aston, not only have we witnessed you with Ms Harris, we have had it confirmed by her. We know you have been seeing each other for some time."

He screwed his face up, like a child about to cry. "I wondered why she wasn't returning my calls or messages."

"So, now you admit to the relationship?"

He hung his head. "Yes."

"Why did you try to hide it from us?"

"It isn't what you think." His eyes flew to her face. "Things were difficult between Michaela and Philip. He hadn't wanted the pregnancy, at least at first. He spent a lot of time out of the house when she needed him most. He wasn't supporting her the way he should have done. I started out as the shoulder she cried on. It developed from there. Neither of us went looking for it."

"And you hid it from us because?"

"Because we knew how it would look. Michaela didn't ask him to take out a massive insurance policy. It's been like a millstone around our necks, and the insurance company are heavily suspicious of his taking it out when he did, only six weeks before he died. They are unlikely to release money anytime soon, and Michaela has this baby coming. She is pregnant, on her own, and receiving very little income in the form of Universal Credit. She didn't even get that until a week ago. I am helping her out. Or, I was, until you lot got to her. She seems to have cut off all communication with me. I expect that's the guilt. She loved him, you know. You're wasting your time if you think we had a hand in Philip's death. Neither myself, nor Michaela, would have wished him ill. I liked the guy, apart from his neglect of Michaela. I had no reason to harm him. That's it. Can I go now?"

"Yes." Yvonne nodded. "You can go."

He looked at her, open-mouthed, as though expecting her to say no.

"This will all pass." She rose from her seat. "And, perhaps, you and Michaela will find happiness."

"Thank you," he replied, eyes narrowed as though expecting a 'but'.

None came.

∽

"Seriously?" Dewi asked as they walked back to CID, his brow furrowed.

"What?"

"You, giving them your blessing."

"Why not? Whatever they may or may not have done together, Dewi, I don't believe them responsible for her partner's death. I genuinely wish them happiness, and she has a baby coming. I want the child to be happy, too. They are human, Dewi. Human relationships are complex. Having an affair does not make you a murderer. This case is far bigger than them, I'm sure of it."

Dewi grinned at her. "Funnily enough, I trust you. I think you are mad as a box of frogs, but I trust your judgement."

"Good, well, we're off to meet with the wives of the pilots killed in the Clywedog Dam crash. It will be hard, but necessary, if we are to get to the bottom of what's going on."

"Understood."

22

PATTERN OR COINCIDENCE

Yvonne and Dewi pulled up outside of a semi-detached property on Barnfields in Newtown. Sharon and Kevin Tranchard's home. Sharon Tranchard had agreed to leave her three children with her mother, while they discussed her dead husband.

Her car pulled up, just as they reached her garden gate, and they walked the garden path together.

"Thank you for meeting us, Mrs Tranchard," Yvonne said as Sharon put her key in the door. "I know this has been an awful time, and that officers have already questioned you."

Sharon led them through the hall, running her hand through her shoulder-length, auburn hair

She sighed. "The kids are heartbroken, and I feel lost without him. Thank God, for the kids. I have to keep going for them."

"Of course." The DI nodded.

"You do," Dewi agreed. "Never think about giving up."

"Are you eating properly?" Yvonne asked.

Sharon nodded. "Small amounts, but I am eating. I

make the meals for the children. I'm amazed at how resilient they are." She smiled, though her mouth had only the barest curl, and her eyes glistened with the tears she was holding back.

She motioned them into her lounge, and to the sofa. "Sorry about the toys. I'm afraid it's a case of having to find somewhere safe to put your feet in our house."

Yvonne grinned. "I love it. Don't knock it. They grow up so fast," she said, thinking of her niece and nephew. "I wanted to ask you about your husband's behaviour, leading up to the crash."

"His behaviour?" Sharon tilted her head.

"Did his demeanour change at all, in the weeks or months before the incident?"

Sharon rubbed her ear, looking into space. "I didn't notice any major change in him, aside from his being quiet."

"Quiet?"

"Lost in his own thoughts. The children noticed he wasn't as playful with them, too."

"How long was this going on for?"

"Oh, I'd say a few weeks, at least. I put it down to his having a lot of pressure and extra duties at work. He loved his job, but it sometimes took a lot out of him."

"I see." Yvonne nodded. "Did you ask him about it? His job, or why he was quiet?"

"Not, specifically, No. I would cuddle him and, well, he wasn't as responsive as he had been. He seemed preoccupied. Again, I put it down to work, so I didn't quiz him."

"I see."

"I felt like it, though."

"Sorry? Felt like what?"

"Quizzing him. But, I didn't want to make it worse. He was spending a lot of time on his phone and sighing. Whatever he was reading was making him unhappy or, at least, irritating him."

"Did you find out what he was viewing on his phone?"

"No. You know what social media is like. Full of all sorts. Some good. Some bad."

"And he was definitely on social media?"

"Yes. I could see the screen, at a distance, even if I couldn't read any of it. I worried he was getting bored with family life."

"Did you ever consider him at risk of suicide? I'm sorry to ask you that, but it is important for us to know."

"No. I can honestly say, I never suspected that. I mean, we all get down, don't we? But he said nothing about that to me, and there was nothing to say he might want to harm himself."

"And he didn't leave you any notes, or anything like that, on the day he died?"

"No, none." Sharon stared at the DI, wide-eyed. "Do you think he knew he was in danger?"

"I don't know." Yvonne sighed. "It's possible. However, we have nothing to suggest that."

"Of course."

"Is there anything else you can think of that might help us, Mrs Tranchard?"

"Not really, no."

Yvonne handed her a card. "Well, if you think of anything, please contact me."

Sharon nodded. "I will, Inspector."

∽

They met Chloe Yates at Maldwyn Sports Center in Newtown, where she had been for her daily workout.

"It helps take my mind off everything," she explained, as they caught up with her in the main atrium. She was feeding the vending machine, looking for a suitable snack.

"Where's the best place for us to talk?" Yvonne asked, looking around for somewhere quieter than reception.

"Through there." Chloe pointed to a room containing tables and chairs, and a viewing window over the swimming pool. "Hardly anyone uses that room. Less disturbance."

As they seated themselves, Yvonne's eyes wandered to the viewing window. The pool was empty, save one lone swimmer clocking up lengths. She pulled out her notes, laying them on the table in front. "First, let me say how sorry we are about your loss, Ms Yates. I know this last couple of weeks must have been painful, and I am sorry we have to intrude on that grief."

Chloe nodded, pulling a handkerchief from a pocket in her joggers. "It's all right. I'm so grateful that you are still looking into Tom's death. A mid-air collision is something I never imagined happening to him. He was always so careful. Meticulous. I've been over and over it in my mind, and something isn't right about what happened. I don't accept that he didn't see the other plane, or that he took his eye off the ball. I used to get uptight about him being so slow and thorough."

Yvonne nodded. "I understand you'd had difficulties?"

Chloe sighed. "We split up a few times. We always got back together. It was a typical case of couldn't live with, couldn't live without." She looked over at the window, tears welling in her eyes. "Now, I have no choice."

The DI put a hand on her arm. "I'm sorry."

Chloe sniffed. "Thanks."

"You told officers, previously, that you had nearly split

up again, a week before the crash. What impact did that have on his mood?"

"It was his idea." Chloe rubbed the back of her neck. "We'd been arguing a lot the previous two days, and he suggested another break. We made up that night, though, so he didn't go."

"Did you get the impression he might purposely hurt himself?"

"What? Do you mean suicide? God, no. Never. He wouldn't do that. Tom would never have done that."

"Did he talk to anyone on social media about flying?"

"His close friends, yes, frequently. He had photos on his page, but he rarely discussed flying with anyone he didn't know really well, only with his flying buddies."

"I see."

"Were you thinking he might have caused the accident on purpose?" Chloe frowned.

"As you know, we have to investigate all avenues. But, as I understand it, he had no history of depressive illness and no physical problems."

"No, none. He kept himself in good shape. He used to come here, to the gym, three times a week. Mentally, he was strong. He deleted one of his social media accounts recently. I don't know why. He reinstated it a few days later. He said there were evil people around. I quizzed him about it, but he didn't say anymore and, like I said, he reinstated his account."

"What about the morning of his fatal flight, was there anything unusual about it? Anything different from his normal routine? Was he more or less affectionate than usual, for example?"

Chloe shook her head. "No. He gave me a quick hug and

a peck on the lips, same as he always did. Said he would be back about teatime."

"Teatime, being?"

"Between five and five-thirty."

"Okay. Anything else you can think of, Ms Yates?"

Chloe shook her head. "Nothing, Inspector."

"Well, thank you for talking to us and for your time." Yvonne and Dewi rose from their seats.

The DI handed Ms Yates her card. "Call me, if you think of anything."

"Thank you. I will."

23

A WALK IN THE WILDERNESS

"What are you up to, Inspector Giles?" Tasha unclipped her seatbelt, narrowing her eyes as the DI parked the car in a lay-by. "Don't get me wrong, I love an excursion to the middle of nowhere as much as the next person, but this one took a while to get to." She grinned. "What have you got up your sleeve?"

Yvonne laughed, throwing off her own seatbelt. "Doctor Phillips, you know me far too well."

"Well, come on then, what are we doing? Besides going for a walk in the wilderness?"

"I've brought you to the site of a fatal air collision that took place between a military jet and light aircraft. A Cessna."

Tasha frowned. "Right."

"I wanted to walk and think about the case we're working on, and run ideas past you, if that is okay. Also, when I came here the other day, the landscape blew me away, and I thought it would be nice to bring you here to see it with me. There is no-one I would rather walk it with."

"Is that right?" Tasha held out her hand.

"Absolutely." Yvonne placed her hand in Tasha's.

"Then, let's go."

The DI shouldered a small rucksack and led her partner over a stile, through the field at the foot of the hill where the military jet impacted the ground.

The small bunch of flowers was now entirely rust-coloured. A dried-up remnant. A shadow of the tribute it had been. The message of love, left in a semi-sealed plastic bag, had smudged in a haze of condensation.

"Six people lost their lives, Tasha. Two in the Cessna and four in the jet." Yvonne shook her head, her eyes travelling the length of the blackened gouge in the hillside.

"What happened?" Tasha turned to face the DI. "Why did they collide?"

Yvonne explained the circumstances, everything the farmer had told them.

"Is he sure of what he saw? The Cessna was waiting for the jet?"

"Yes, as it had done on prior occasions."

"So, what do you think happened? A suicidal pilot, wanting to end it all via a speeding jet?" Tasha tilted her head. "Only, that makes no sense. I mean, why would you commit suicide that way, knowing you would kill not only the other person in your plane, but innocent others in the other craft. Why not just plow your plane into the ground, or the hillside? You wouldn't need to collide with another aircraft. Sounds crazy."

Yvonne nodded. "And it is. But, if Carl Evans is right, either the pilot, or his right-hand man, wanted that collision."

"Wait, are you thinking terrorism?"

Yvonne nodded. "If I'm honest, yes, it is one option. They murdered an AAIB inspector last week. His name was

Gethin Jenkins, and he was working with us on this case. I thought he was up to something and he would have confessed to me, in private. He never got the chance. In his notes, he had written the phrase, Hand of Darkness, and emphatically underlined it. What if that is the name of some sort of terror organisation, who killed Jenkins because he had something on them?"

"Okay. I'm with you, but wouldn't a terror organisation have made themselves known or made some demands by now? Have you looked them up? Is there such a group?"

"Counter-terrorism have never heard of them, and we could find nothing on the internet, either nationally or internationally."

"Well, it is an odd sort of terror group that doesn't even try to bring attention to itself, nor have aims, and demands." Tasha shook her head. "Unless they haven't come forward, yet, because they are waiting for something."

"You will think I'm going a little crazy." Yvonne grimaced. "But, what if they are gathering information on pilots and government officials, and using it to force them to commit acts of sabotage, or worse?"

"You mean digging up personal information?"

"Yes. Before he died, I was convinced Gethin Jenkins had been getting rid of evidence. Clearing up the trail for someone. What would make him do that?"

"Fear of exposure, fear of harm to himself or to a loved one-"

"Exactly. I don't know who, or what, the Hand of Darkness is, but my gut tells me it's linked to the deaths of all these men."

"Well, if you're right, the group will make themselves know to us, soon." Tasha frowned. "I have an important question."

"Go on."

"How do you make someone commit an act that will cause the loss of their own life? Death is worse than exposure, surely?"

"Unless they didn't think they would die. What if they meant these events to cause the demise of others and not themselves, or perhaps these flights were meant to achieve something else that shouldn't have resulted in crashes at all? What if their missions went wrong?"

Might be worth looking into near misses that have resulted in no crash, or only one plane, crashing. See if you can identify a pattern between any that you find and your own cases." Tasha placed a hand on the DI's arm. "Could open up fresh leads for you."

Yvonne nodded. "Good thinking, I might do that."

"Wait." Tasha swung Yvonne round to face her. "You said they murdered the AAIB inspector."

"Yes."

The psychologist's eyes flicked over her partner's face, then held her gaze. "Are you in danger?"

"No." Yvonne shook her head. "Why would I be? Gethin knew what was going on. Me? I don't have a clue. What have they got to be afraid of?" She gave Tasha a grin. "I'm safe enough, for now."

Tasha smiled. "Don't get in any planes until you have whoever is responsible in the can."

"I won't." Yvonne squeezed Tasha's hand. "Or, wander under any bridges in Builth."

"What?"

"Where Gethin was murdered."

"Oh, I see. Well, make sure that you don't."

"Shall we find somewhere to eat our lunch?" The DI leaned her head on Tasha's shoulder as they walked.

Tasha hugged her close. "Yes, let's."

~

Royston looked over his Piper sitting idle in the Hangar.

It was its fifth anniversary. Five years since he used his savings, plus a substantial loan, to buy it. It still made his heart beat faster.

He had kept the paintwork pristine and, with regular cleaning, it looked as good as it ever had. His pride and joy. Karen had never quite understood his attachment to it, or why he referred to it as 'she'. It just seemed right.

His stomach muscles clenched til they hurt, squeezing the air out of him as he contemplated what he would soon have to do. It wasn't just the threat of exposure for an offence he hadn't committed; it was the unspoken threat. The knives. Karen. A murdered AAIB inspector had been all over the news. Royston was sure he knew who was responsible, and they would think nothing of doing the same to him and, or, his wife. He couldn't risk that.

If he spoke to police, would they believe him? Or, would they believe he'd been having a relationship with an underage girl? That kind of shit stuck. Even if found not guilty, everyone would still think he did it. No smoke without fire and all that. How could he prove nothing had taken place? Given their messages. Messages he would not have sent if he had even an inkling she was underage. *If* she was underage. He had no proof that she was. He rubbed his forehead. Fear mashed his head. Nothing made sense.

Karen appeared in his mind's eye, her face contorted with anguished disappointment. She'd believe them, of course. She accused him of being distant. This would confirm it. For her, it would all fit.

He couldn't tell her the truth about the girl, and he couldn't let them tell her, either. He couldn't watch Karen's love turn to hate. And, if they hurt her?

The first time he ever laid eyes on her, was at someone's twenty-first birthday party. A person he barely knew. He hadn't intended going to the bash, but his mate, Mike, persuaded him. He would always be grateful to Mike.

He first saw her studying him via a mirror. Caught her looking. Her hand trembled when he shook it. Her tilted head, her open mouth, and the graceful line of her neck, had him forgetting the rest of the room. They, alone, were at the party. All else was background. For them, it was instantaneous attraction.

It was rare, what they had. He had felt it then. He knew it now.

Life would be pointless without her. They might have suffered from boredom, of late, but he loved her. He didn't tell her often enough. He would change that. If anything happened to him, she needed to know how much he cared. The love of his life. Forever.

24

AN AWKWARD GAIT

Yvonne parked at Welshpool Airport, having come on her own, to speak again with Tim Payne. The mid-afternoon sun hurt her eyes as she got out of her vehicle, heading into the hangar.

"Good to see you again, Inspector." He held out his hand. It smelled of fresh soap, contrasting with his grease-ridden overalls.

"And you, Mr Payne." She gave his hand a firm shake.

"You wanted to talk to me?" he asked, eyebrows raised. "It sounded urgent."

"It is." The DI's brow furrowed. "Do you have a rota of scheduled flights, covering the next couple of months? And, do you have unscheduled flights?"

"We have many flights in and out, much of them unscheduled." Payne scratched his head. "They come from all over the country. Sometimes, these include vintage warplanes. You never know what will come over the horizon. Could be news crews in helicopters, even modern jets. We see it all."

"Oh." She rubbed her forehead. "I didn't realise it was so irregular."

"Why?" he asked, tilting his head. "What do you want a rota for?"

"I wanted to look through it." Yvonne coughed into her hand, to avoid his seeing the colour rising in her cheeks. She was too embarrassed to tell him she was trying to identify 'at risk' flights. She suspected it would be a thankless task, and her chances of being able of finding them, even with a rota, would be slim-to-none.

"Ah, Rob." Tim waved at the silhouette entering the hangar, and grinned at the DI. "My errant son returns. He should be in college this afternoon, but told them he was ill."

Yvonne watched as the young man of around seventeen or eighteen, made his way over to them. As he approached, something struck her as familiar.

"Do you have CCTV?" she asked.

"We have web cams on the airfield, why?"

"How often is your son here?"

"Pretty regularly. Why do you ask?"

"Keen on aviation?" She forced a smile, as Rob joined them.

"Rob, you remember DI Giles, don't you?" Tim said, welcoming his son.

Rob did not answer. Instead, he stared at her, his face motionless.

Tim Payne cleared his throat. "Will there be anything else, Inspector?"

"No, that will be all, thank you."

As she left, her mind raced. Ideas and questions came almost faster than she could process them. She had to get back to the team.

∼

"Uh oh," Callum grinned. "Watch out, Dewi, she's onto something."

Yvonne stuck out her tongue, smiling despite herself. "You know, I think I am."

"Really?" Dewi sighed. "I'm glad one of us is. You will not like this."

"Like what?" She frowned. "What am I not going to like?"

"The DCI has been in. He wants to see you. From his face, it's not good news." Dewi scratched his stubble. "Sorry, I know you've only just got in."

"Could you do me a favour?" Yvonne perched on the end of Dewi's desk.

"Sure. What do you want?"

"Can you look up Rob, or Robert, Payne on social media. Check them all: Facebook, Instagram, Twitter etc. Anything he might be into as a mature teenager. He's Tim Payne's son, and an aviation enthusiast. He lives in Welshpool with his parents."

"Okay."

"Have a look at whatever is in the public domain, find out who is friends are, and look at their profiles, too."

"Ma'am? What are you up to?"

She pursed her lips. "There's something about the way he walks and holds himself. It reminded me of the figure on the river path in Builth. Also, can you get the river path footage ready to view again, so I can look at it when I finish with the DCI. I want to be sure of my facts before we wade in."

Dewi nodded, his eyes bright. "Will do. Good luck in there."

"Thanks. I have a feeling I'll need it."

∽

"Yvonne, come in. How is it going, out in the jungle?" He motioned her to take a seat, pulling up a chair.

"You want to see me?"

"I do. I went through the material you gathered about the air collisions."

"And?"

"There's nothing in it that would make me change my mind. I still feel that the AAIB are best-placed to investigate them."

"But-"

"Seriously, there's no evidence of any unlawful activity, in what you've given me. I admit, there is some circumstantially interesting material but, again, it's not enough to warrant investigation by us. We can leave it to the Air Accident Investigations."

Yvonne shook her head.

"I am happy for you to assist Llandod CID with the inquiry into Gethin Jenkins' death. That's it."

Yvonne stood. "What if I had a more concrete link between the air collisions and Gethin's murder?"

"Have you?" Llewelyn raised his eyebrows. "I thought you gave me everything?"

She sighed. "I revisited Welshpool Airport today, and I may have a suspect for Gethin's murder, but I need to view the CCTV footage from the river path again and trawl through social media."

"Who?" The DCI frowned.

"I went to see Tim Payne and, looking at his son Rob, I

realized he bears an amazing resemblance to the figure we saw in the footage. I think he could be our killer."

"Did Llandod find the knife used on Gethin?"

Yvonne shook her head. "No, the weapon hasn't been found. Hence, there are no fingerprints for comparison. I think the killer kept the weapon. It's likely in his kitchen drawer."

"I see. We wouldn't get a conviction on the CCTV evidence on its own. The image simply isn't good enough. There isn't a clear view of the face inside the hood. If, however, you were to find the murder weapon-"

"I know. Having seen Rob Payne today, though, I believe his movements match with the person in the footage. Do I have your permission to chase up his social media and, if needs be, get a warrant for his phone and computers, and his private messages?"

Llewelyn stared at her, holding his chin. "Are you arresting him on suspicion of Jenkins' murder?"

"Maybe."

"I'd be sticking my neck out, if you're wrong. He, or his family, could sue us."

"I know."

"How sure are you that it's him?"

"I'd say seventy-five to eighty percent. That could rise, if we find something on his phone or in his social media that supports it."

A knock on the door made her jump.

"Come in." The DCI ordered, in a clipped tone, his eyes still on Yvonne.

Dewi peered around the door. "Sorry to disturb you both. I thought you'd want to see this. We've got video footage of Rob Payne and his friends on a walkabout. It's good footage of Payne for comparison. I have to say, I think his movements and his clothing are very similar to what we see on the Builth footage. Callum has it on his screen, if you want to see for yourselves."

Yvonne and the DCI made a scramble for the door. The DI caught her skirt on a chair which crashed to the floor, almost taking out Llewelyn.

"Try to make it in one piece, guys." Dewi laughed.

∼

Callum started the video.

No-one said a word as they watched the clips side-by-side, flicking their eyes between the two.

"Look at his top." Yvonne pointed at the screen.

Callum froze the videos.

"Look at the top of his right shoulder. The light patch. Does everyone agree it looks the same in each clip, in shape and shade?"

Dewi peered at the screen. "I'd say they look identical and, comparing for the second time, there is little doubt in my mind that we are seeing the same male in both clips. The gait and swagger are the same. The build is right, the stride, everything. I think we are watching Gethin Jenkins' killer joking about with his friends."

The DCI ran his hands through his hair. "Okay, I've seen enough to agree to pulling him in for questioning. We'll get a warrant for seizure of his property, if we've a good enough reason to arrest him on suspicion. If you get something from him in interview, that will help. I doubt we could get a conviction on the CCTV footage alone, but I agree he is a viable suspect."

Yvonne stepped back. "Dai, call Llandod CID and let them know what we've found. Ask if they can get someone down here in the next hour or two. Likely, they'll want to be in on the interview, and we won't have that long to question him, if we don't get more evidence, or a confession."

Dai nodded. "I'll get onto them."

"In the meantime, Callum, could you get me the names of all the friends identified in the social media video? We should talk to some of them as well."

"Will do."

"Well done, Yvonne. Good work." Llewelyn tapped her on the arm.

"Thanks." She smiled, wondering why getting him to this point had been so hard. "Does that mean we get to stay with the air crash investigations?"

The DCI nodded. "For now. His strong links with local aviation make that the sensible option. I'll review it in two days. I have every faith in you, Yvonne. If anyone can figure this out, you can."

"Thank you, sir."

25

A DIFFICULT TIME

Royston watched his wife reading in the armchair opposite, her glasses perched halfway down her nose. She was far away, lost in some world or other. He didn't have the heart to tell her how much he longed for her to come back to him. To live in the moment with him. She would want to know why he asked for this, when he had never done so before, and he wouldn't be able to tell her.

His eyes wandered over her straw-coloured hair, her pale blue eyes behind the lenses, and the freckles over her nose. His chest swelled with love for her.

They had had their moments, their rows, their wobbles, but he adored her. She had stayed with him through everything. That was commitment. That was what he had risked with his foolishness over some girl he didn't even know. It took the threat of imminent loss for him to see this with absolute clarity.

A pebble-sized lump clogged in his throat. The hour was coming. He would take his plane and fly it at someone else's. Some poor, unsuspecting sod, who wouldn't see it coming.

Sure, they would see his aircraft and take evasive action, but they would not expect him to turn and come at them again. Aiming for the near miss.

It would be in the hands of providence, the outcome unpredictable. They might read it right, and avoid him, or panic and turn the wrong way, making a collision unavoidable.

He shuddered. It would leave Karen a widow, and the family of the other pilot, grief-stricken. He would devastate an untold number of people's lives. Lives that would take a long time to stitch back together, even if that was possible.

He coughed, to clear his throat, and Karen looked up, an accusation in those piercing blue eyes, her furrowed brow informing him of his intrusion into a good bit.

He didn't blame her. She did not understand the importance of the moment they were in. How could she? Royston walked to the back of her chair and massaged her shoulders. A quiet message of love and reassurance as much for himself as for his wife.

"I love you." It was simple, and it was complicated. He invested it with more meaning than anything he had uttered for years.

Karen sighed. "I love you, too." She tossed the sentence at him, her eyes remaining on the book. Throwaway words. Throwaway lives.

Tears pricked his eyes as he left her to her reading, heading to the kitchen to put the kettle on.

∼

Dewi found Yvonne in the office. "He's here, ma'am."

Yvonne nodded. "Good. Ready to interview?"

Dewi shook his head. "He's still waiting on the duty solicitor. His dad is in the waiting room."

Yvonne gathered her notes, photographs, and snippets of the social media posts Callum had printed for her. "I'm good to go, Dewi. Just let me know as soon as the duty solicitor is free."

∽

Yvonne did the introductions and pointed out the camera to the suspect.

Rob Payne frowned at it, folding his arms, a sullen expression on his face. He spread his legs wide under the table. Now and then, his foot kicked the leg of her chair.

She moved her seat backwards. "Can you put your hood down for us, please, Mr Payne? Can I call you Rob?"

He shrugged.

The duty solicitor sorted through paperwork. Yvonne waited for him to catch up.

"Rob, where were you on Thursday, seventh of November?"

He shrugged. "Don't know. Thursday's a college day. I was probably in college." He kept his arms folded across his chest and sank lower in his chair. His foot was once again touching the leg of her chair.

Yvonne made a point of looking at her notes. "According to your social media, you skipped off college that day, intending to hang out with your friends."

"Then, I was probably walking or hanging with my mates, like it said in the post."

"We're talking two weeks ago, Rob. Think back. Where were you in the afternoon, exactly two weeks ago?"

He chewed the inside of his cheek, jiggling his foot

against her chair leg. He moved his hands to the front pocket of his hoodie. "I was walking in the country."

"Where?"

He shrugged. "Up by the dams, I think."

"Would that be Llyn Clywedog?"

His eyes darted to hers, scrutinising her. "By Hafren Forest."

"Did you go across to Builth Wells?"

"No." He shook his head, his eyes on the table.

"I want you to watch something with us, Rob. It's CCTV footage taken from the river path in Builth on the seventh of November."

Rob looked at his solicitor.

"Your solicitor hasn't seen this, yet." Yvonne informed him, pressing play on the video. She paused it on the clearest shot they had. "Recognise the person in this clip, Rob?"

He glared at her. "That's not me."

"No? Do you know who it might be?"

"No."

"We think it is you, and that the clip shows you before, and after, you murdered a man underneath the bridge."

"Wait a minute, you can't-" Rob's solicitor protested.

Yvonne held up her hand. "Please bear with us, I have another clip to play for you."

The solicitor fell silent.

As the second clip played, Rob sank even lower in his seat, his foot vibrating her chair leg.

"Here we have a group of friends walking along a country road. Who is this person?" She pointed to Payne on the screen. "We got this from your social media."

"You can't do that, it's private." Rob pouted.

"No. All of this was public and freely accessible. Anyone

can view anything you put on your wall, at anytime, if you don't alter your privacy settings to friends-only. Surely, you knew that?"

He made no reply.

"This is you, isn't it, Rob?"

His eyes fixed on the desk and he maintained his silence.

"I'm looking at your walk, your swagger, the roll of your hips, the length of your stride, and the markings on your hooded top, and I see a striking resemblance between the figures on these two clips. What do you think? Where is that Hoodie, Rob? Do you still have it?"

Rob's solicitor pointed his pen at the DI. "Are you accusing my client of murder? Because, if you are, you'd better have more than this CCTV footage. I do not see a clearly identifiable face on the clip."

"We've applied for a warrant to search your home, Rob. We'll be going through your phone and any laptop, or other computers, you may have. We'll be going through your clothing, and your mother's kitchen drawers. In the meantime, since you cannot satisfactorily explain where you were on the seventh of November, I am arresting you on suspicion of the murder of Mr Gethin Jenkins." She cautioned him, before excusing herself from the room.

Dewi left with her, to make Rob and his solicitor a cup of tea.

She caught up with the DCI in his office.

"Yvonne, I'm waiting for the go ahead from the court-"

She held up a hand. "No need, thank you, I've arrested him on suspicion. We can seize whatever we need to"

"You've arrested him?"

"Well, he has no alibi, and no satisfactory account of his whereabouts at the time of Gethin's death. I've arrested him for the murder, and I'm hoping we'll get enough from the search to charge him. We may get lucky and find the weapon or bloodied clothing. There could be private messages, too, between him and his friends. My gut feeling is that they are visiting these crash sites after the fact."

"Really?"

"Payne admitted being with his friends near Clywedog. The time and date correspond with the air crash. I think it likely we'll be arresting his friends, at some point. If Dai has their identities, I think I will bring them all in for questioning. Dai can team up with uniform."

"Right." Llewelyn nodded. "I trust you to get on with it, then. There's an officer on the way from Llandod. Should be with you in the next hour. Keep me informed of progress."

"Thanks, sir."

∽

Royston ate half of his lunch of tuna and sweetcorn sandwiches, made by his wife. Whilst not what he would have requested, had he been on death row, they tasted good. He mused about what his last meal of choice would have been, and decided it would be lamb curry, hot, with rice, naan, and poppadoms.

He smiled to himself. Wistful. Tuna and sweetcorn, prepared by his wife, would do just fine.

Half of his Piper gleamed. The polish and leather lay on the ground, waiting for him to finish the other half. If he went out today, at least he would go out in a shiny plane. Except, he would not go out. He had decided it. This would be his lucky day. He would keep his wits about him and his head clear, reading and preparing for every manoeuvre the other pilot made.

He wondered, not for the first time, if he should tell the

police. Give them everything, and risk losing his wife. Maybe they would believe him about the girl. Maybe they wouldn't. Too many maybes. Not enough certainty. He didn't trust, maybe. He had to go ahead. Leave his fate to providence.

26

HAND OF DARKNESS

"Who are the Hand of Darkness?"

Payne glowered at her, pupils dilated, nostrils flared. "No comment."

"Is it you?"

"No comment."

"Is it your mates and you?"

"No comment."

"What did you have on Gethin Jenkins?"

"No comment."

"Why did you kill him?"

"No comment."

"Was it because you knew he would talk to me?"

"No comment."

"But, you knew he would talk, didn't you?"

"No comment."

"He told you he'd had enough."

"No comment."

"Perhaps, your friends will be more communicative?"

"No comment."

"I think you had a hand in several air disasters."

"No comment."

"Collisions which resulted in eleven deaths."

"No comment."

"I think you and your gang are the Hand of Darkness, so-called because you are the instigators of whatever caused those accidents."

"No comment."

"Was it blackmail? Did you blackmail pilots, like you blackmailed Jenkins?"

"No comment."

"You're going too far." Rob's solicitor warned.

"Oh really? I don't think I'm going far enough. Interview suspended, one-fifteen."

Yvonne left the interview room to look for Callum. "Any sign of the Llandrindod Wells guy, yet?"

He shook his head. "Got a call about five minutes ago, saying he would be fifteen minutes. He should be here within the next ten minutes, or so."

Yvonne nodded. "Great. Show him to the interview room when he gets here. Have you heard from Dai?"

"Not yet, but there was a commotion down in the yard, earlier. Several vans returning with, I suspect, your chap's friends. There's a lot of bagged stuff, too."

"Good. Give me a shout when Dai gets back."

"Will do."

∽

DI PHIL MASON arrived with his tie hanging loose, a mac over his arm, and a brown leather case with a broken strap that flapped as he walked. He wore his glasses on top of his head and, at first glance, Yvonne had concerns.

His handshake was solid, however, and he spoke with a quiet intelligence and a firm, even tone.

She liked him. "Nice to meet you, Phil. We haven't met before, have we? I'm Yvonne Giles."

"Nice to meet you, too. We haven't met. I came here from Manchester five months ago." He smiled. "I hear you've got a suspect for our murder?"

"We do. I suggest you look at the video footage we have before you interview him. We think it's the guy we are holding, and we have arrested him on suspicion. I have officers out seizing his property and bringing in his friends."

Yvonne's phone pinged.

It was Dai, unusually breathless and high-pitched. "We found a large biscuit barrel in Payne's back garden. Someone's been burning clothes in it. SOCO are photographing and bagging the remnants for forensics. Could be the clothing he wore for Gethin's murder. The colour of the remnants would match. A luminol test on one piece of the clothing lit it up like a Christmas tree, under UV."

"So, he's been burning bloody clothes. I knew it."

"Yes, forensics said they'll make this a priority, and run DNA tests as soon as they can. They reckon they could get the results to us within four-to-five hours."

"What about mobile phone, laptop, knives?"

"We've bagged a phone and laptop. Only one phone found, though, and I'm afraid it's not the number Gethin called, on the afternoon of his death. Oh, and we have bagged all the knives from the kitchen drawer."

"Good work, Dai. We will continue working on Payne. Text me any developments. I'll check my messages whenever I can."

"Will do, ma'am. You should know, we've brought in two guys and a female. They're the friends we saw Payne with in the clip at Clywedog dam. Do you want me to get everything ready for their interviews?"

"Yes, please. Check their ages. Make sure they have counsel."

"I've explained they are to be questioned in connection with a murder, but they are not under arrest."

"Good. We don't know that they have committed any offence, we've got little-to-nothing from Payne. He's doing the 'no comment' thing. If you find anything with 'Hand of Darkness' written in it, let me know immediately."

"Right you are, ma'am."

∼

DI MASON WATCHED the video clip in silence, save for the odd, "hmm."

"What do you think?" Yvonne asked, after he had watched everything several times.

"I'd say you've made a good call. From what I see, he's a good match for the river path suspect. What's he said?"

Yvonne gave Mason a rundown of the interview so far, and finished with, "And he's closed down. He started saying, 'no comment' right after I bought up Gethin Jenkins' murder. He was talking until that point, though he wasn't saying very much."

"Right, I'll have a go with him." Mason puffed out his meagre chest and picked up his ailing briefcase.

∼

MELISSA HINES, aged seventeen years and six months, sat in the interview room, her arms folded. Her dark hair hung in waves around her elfin face. Now and then, she chewed the ends of it, twirling them around in her fingers, scowling at the DI.

Her solicitor finished writing his notes and put his pen down.

Yvonne placed her papers and a few crash photographs on the table, taking her seat opposite the girl. "Hello Melissa. Is it okay for me to call you Melissa? My name is DI Yvonne Giles. How are you?"

Melissa made no answer.

"You are probably wondering why we brought you in here today-"

"Am I under arrest?" Melissa interrupted her. "Because, if you're not arresting me, I want to go. You can't keep me here."

Yvonne pursed her lips. "We can keep you for a little while. We would like to talk to you in connection with a murder that happened in Builth Wells, two weeks ago."

"Murder?" She jerked her head back, staring wide-eyed at the DI.

"Yes. Murder."

"Wait a minute, I ain't murdered nobody."

"I'm not saying you have, Melissa, but we believe you know the person who did."

"Wait, what?"

"In a moment, we will show you footage taken of the person we believe murdered Gethin Jenkins on the river path in Builth Wells. I want you to look closely at it and tell me if you recognise the person in the film."

Melissa flicked a look at her solicitor, who nodded in response.

Yvonne pressed play, and they watched in silence as the river path video unfolded.

"Would you like to see it again?" Yvonne asked.

Melissa shook her head.

"Do you recognise the person in the clip?"

"No." She flicked her solicitor another look.

"Are you sure? A man lost his life. Somewhere in the middle of that footage, while that suspect was under the bridge, our victim had his throat slit. He bled out over the path, the verge, and the underside of the bridge."

Melissa put her hand to her mouth, as though suppressing a gag. "Yeah, I told you. I'm sure."

"I think you recognise the suspect. I think he is a friend of yours."

"It's not Rob, if that's what you're thinking."

"Rob? Rob who?"

"No-one. I don't know who it is."

"We were thinking along the lines that it was a Rob or Robert, so we popped along to his house, and guess what? We found items of clothing that someone had tried to burn. They weren't very successful. They left remnants of clothing in a tin in the garden. We've taken samples for DNA testing. Were you there? Did you help Rob in his attempt to get rid of evidence?"

"No."

"Rob, or someone he knows, tried to burn bloodied clothing. Are you sure you didn't help?"

"Yes."

"Really?"

"Look, I wasn't there when they..." Melissa fell silent, rolling her eyes and throwing her head back.

"I think you're trying to lead my client." The solicitor interjected.

Yvonne gave him a look. "Who's they, Melissa? Who was it that helped Rob get rid of bloodied clothing?"

Melissa shrugged.

"Matt Jakes? Simon Jones? Are they the ones you were referring too? Was it the boys who went around to help Rob?"

"I don't know what you're talking about."

"Who are the Hand of Darkness?"

"I don't know."

"Is that your gang?"

"I don't know."

"You don't know? That's a strange answer."

"You are badgering my client." Melissa's solicitor leaned forward, as though about to stand up.

The DI addressed him. "This is a murder investigation. These questions are necessary. We may be talking more than one murder, here."

He stared at her, eyes widening, taken aback by the last.

"Melissa," Yvonne continued, "We'll have the DNA results back, soon. I have a feeling they will show that the blood came from the murdered Air Accident Investigation Bureau inspector, Gethin Jenkins. If it proves to be his blood, we could charge you with aiding and abetting, if we find your DNA is also present. If you know anything, or are withholding information, I suggest you have a rethink. Tell us what you know."

"I don't know anything."

"I believe Mr Jenkins was murdered because he was looking into these crashes." Yvonne placed a photograph from each of the recent crash sites in front of the girl, taking her time to make sure she looked at each. "Know anything about these?"

Melissa turned her face away.

"Bad, weren't they? Don't you want a closer look? They're pretty grim."

The girl would not look.

"Very well, Melissa. We'll give you a break; come back in a little while. Interview suspended."

∼

DEWI APPEARED out of interview room two.

"Anything?" Yvonne asked.

"Nothing." He shook his head. "Are you free? Do you want to have a go?"

"Sure." Yvonne was glad she had visited the ladies' room. She had had to cross her legs through most of Melissa's interview. "What about Mason? Is he still in with Payne?"

"As far as I know." Dewi nodded.

Yvonne took a deep breath and went in.

Matt Jakes sat with his legs extended in front, hands in the front pocket of his hoodie. His dark hair, shaved at the back and sides, had thick gel on top.

"Hello Mr Jakes, can I call you Matt?" Yvonne seated herself opposite him.

He shrugged. "Call me what you like."

"I understand my colleague, DS Dewi Hughes has shown you some CCTV footage of the person we think murdered a someone."

Jakes stared at her.

"Do you recognise the person in the footage?"

"Nope." A smile spread across his face, which he stifled with an unconvincing yawn.

"Are you sure?"

"Sure."

"We think it could be a friend of yours."

"Nope."

"Let me show you some further footage." She played the video taken from Rob Payne's social media, then showed him the stills of the figure in question, taken from each clip. "Any similarities between the man in the CCTV footage and in the social media video?"

"I don't see any." He attempted to stifle another grin.

"A man died, Matt. I don't find that funny. So, why do you?"

His face straightened. "I don't know what you're talking about, you're wasting your time asking me these questions."

Yvonne told him of the burned clothing they had found at Rob Payne's place. "Did you help him burn it?"

"No."

"Well, I've just been talking to someone who seems to think you did?"

"What?" His face muscles stiffened; his eyes sparked fire. "Who've you been talking to you?"

"Your friends. The ones walking with you in the video. Which one do you think might have dropped you in it over the clothing?"

"They're lying."

"We're carrying out DNA tests. The results are due any minute."

"I've changed my mind. I want a solicitor."

"Interview suspended."

∽

Yvonne bumped into Mason, as he came out of interview room one. "How is it going in there?"

"Payne's impenetrable. He's saying 'no comment' to everything."

Yvonne nodded. "God, I hope we get some DNA from those clothes. In the meantime, I'll have another go, after I've spoken to his mate, Simon Jones."

"Do you want me to come in with you, when you see Payne?"

"That would be good?" Yvonne smiled. "I see chinks in the armour. We'll keep chipping away at them."

"He'll crack, eventually." Mason smiled back. "Can I ask you a question?"

"Sure."

"Why are we not waiting for the DNA results to come back from the clothing?"

Yvonne sighed. "If these guys have been doing what I think they have, there may be pilots at risk. I don't know how many pilots, or how imminent that risk may be. Ergo, time is of the essence."

Mason's brow furrowed. "What have they been doing?"

"I think this gang have been manipulating, and possibly blackmailing, pilots. I'm not sure how it's all connected, yet, but I believe these youngsters are behind several recent air accidents. Twelve men are dead, eleven of them were pilots. There could be more vulnerable airmen, waiting in the wings, if you pardon the pun."

"I had no idea."

"Hmm. We'll keep working on them. I couldn't forgive myself if we failed to prevent another tragedy."

∼

YVONNE KEPT her chair pushed back from the table, since Simon Jones' long legs stuck out her side. He appeared to be the more approachable of the gang, though still wary. Mousy hair tucked behind his ears, he made decent eye contact with herself and Mason.

"Can you tell me why I'm here?" He asked, after biting on his thumbnail for several seconds.

"Oh, I'm sorry." Yvonne grimaced. "Didn't DS Hughes explain to you?"

He shook his head.

"A man was murdered in Builth Wells, two weeks ago. We believe you are friends with our main suspect."

He eyed her, his mouth falling open, as though he wanted to say something.

She waited, but nothing came.

The DI played the river path CCTV footage.

Jones watched in silence, shuffling in his seat every so often.

"Recognise this person?"

He shook his head.

One of your other friends recognised him. Gave us a name. Yvonne bit her lip. It was the truth, reshaped a little.

"Then why do you need me to identify him?"

"Him? So, it is a male then?"

He shrugged. "You said you had a name."

"If you were to give me a name, what would it be?"

"I don't have a name."

As with Matt Jakes, Yvonne played the social media video.

"Is that your gang?" She asked.

"It's not my gang." He frowned. "I'm not the one in charge."

"Then, who is?"

"No-one."

"You sure?"

"Yeah."

"But you agree you are a part of a gang?"

"We're mates."

"I see. Who, or what, is the Hand of Darkness?"

He sat upright, sweat beading on his forehead.

"Simon? It's okay. You're safe with us."

"Never heard of them," he said, finally.

"You sure about that? You seemed a little worried when I mentioned them."

"I'm sure. Look, what's this all about? I shouldn't be here."

"Do you know anything about a tin with burned clothing in it? We found it in one of your friend's gardens."

He blanched. "No. Why would I?"

"The clothing remnants were covered in blood. Were the clothes yours?"

"No." He shook his head, glancing from her to Mason and back. "I didn't hurt anyone. I wouldn't hurt anyone."

"So, who did? Who was the figure on the river path in Builth, Simon? Did you recognise any of your friends?"

"You'd have to speak to them." He folded his arms.

"Oh, we are. Trust me, we are."

"I need the toilet and a smoke."

Yvonne nodded. "Interview suspended."

27

TIME RUNNING OUT

Royston finished polishing his plane and stepped back to admire the effect. He could see himself in the metal parts, perfectly reflected and bent out of shape. The rest of the plane had never had a sheen like that. He checked his watched. Two hours until his flight. He reached into his satchel and pulled out the rest of his lunch, wrapped in silver foil.

He thought of his wife, and her singing whilst she made his sandwiches and the breakfast pot of tea. She didn't know this might be his last meal. He took a bite, but didn't feel like chewing it.

Tim Payne wandered into the hangar. Whistling, like everything was grand.

Royston watched him, envious.

He thought about the girl. He would never have followed through with her. An affair on his wife was something he had never managed and was never likely to. He loved her too much.

He eyed Payne, momentarily tempted to tell him everything. To unburden himself. To find a way out.

Payne waved at him.

He waved back. Should he? Should he say something?

"Royston." Tim checked his watch. "You're early, aren't you?"

Royston swallowed his mouthful. "I've been giving her a bit of a polish."

Payne cast his eyes over the Piper. "She's looking good, mate. You've given her lots of love there, buddy."

Royston nodded.

"But you've still got over an hour until your flight. What you going to do until then?"

Royston shrugged. "Read. I brought a magazine with me."

Payne placed his hands on his hips. "Well, if you are at a loss, you could help me."

Royston stood up. "Why? What are you up to?"

"My engine is knocking. I thought I'd go through it, check and oil a few bits, and see how it runs. See if it's something the engineers will need a look at."

Royston sucked air through his teeth. "No problem, I didn't really want this food, anyway. Let's look at her."

∾

"No comment." Rob glowered, when the DI returned to the room. "That's all you're gonna get. Save us all some time and let me out of here."

"I can't do that, Rob." She pressed her lips together, scouring his face. "Don't get me wrong, I would love to wrap this up right here and now. But, that all depends on you."

Rob sighed and folded his arms, avoiding looking at her.

She leaned in over the desk. "I'm not letting any of you

go until I've gotten to the bottom of whatever it is your little gang have got going on."

Rob's solicitor held up a hand. "You are intimidating my client, Inspector."

Yvonne leaned back. "Fine. Does your client know how many years he could face?"

"You've got nothing on me or my friends. You're fishing and you know you are."

The DI tapped her fingers on the desk. "It's only a matter of time, until we get those DNA results, Rob. If I'm right, and that is Gethin Jenkins' blood on those clothes, you're looking at life. But, it's not just Jenkins' murder, is it? See, I think Jenkins' death is the tip of the iceberg. I think his death is linked to a bunch of fatal air collisions in the area, and that you are behind them. I may not have all the links, yet, but believe me, I will. And, when I do…"

28

PRESSURE

"Any word on the DNA tests, yet? I thought they could get the answers to us within four hours." Yvonne paced the corridor.

Dewi put a hand on her arm. "They'll get back to us, soon. I'll give them another call in ten minutes, that'll be around the four-hour mark. Seriously, we're lucky they can run this test for us. It's expensive and they don't do them often. They are using an integrated microfluidic system." He grinned, nodding his head and tapping his nose.

"A what?" Yvonne poked him in the ribs. "You've learned that to impress me, haven't you?"

Dewi pulled a face. "I know these things."

"Yeah? Well, what is an integrated microfluidic system? Eh? What the dickens is it, Mr Clever-clogs?"

Dewi narrowed his eyes in a mock knowing look, emphasising the words for effect. "It's integrated... and it's microfluidic."

Yvonne laughed despite herself. "Like I thought. You haven't got a clue. Well, whatever it is, we need it. I really don't want to let Robert Payne go, through lack of evidence."

"We could charge him on the CCTV images."

"Maybe, but I want something concrete for the CPS, and I want to confront Payne with something tangible. I suspect he believes he's done enough to destroy the DNA, and he's happy to hold out until we show him otherwise. *If* we can show him otherwise. Is it time to call forensics, yet?"

"You really are in a hurry for this, aren't you?"

"For all we know, Dewi, there are other pilots being blackmailed, and compromised, by this gang. We don't know if one might be about to take to the skies, do we? And we won't, not until one of this gang breaks. We need that evidence, and we need it now."

∽

"Rob, I have bad news for you." Yvonne flicked a glance at DI Mason, who nodded.

Rob glared at her.

"We've had the DNA results from the lab."

Muscles flickered in his cheek.

She continued. "We have identified the blood on the clothing we found in your garden. Clothing that someone tried to destroy. We think that someone was you. The blood belonged to Gethin Jenkins. Do you have anything you wish to say? I remind you that we have arrested you on suspicion of murder. If you stay silent during questioning, we can inform the courts of your refusal to cooperate, when this goes to trial."

"Can I see a copy of the result?" Rob's solicitor asked. "I'll need time alone with my client."

"And you'll get it, before we question your client regarding Mr Jenkins' murder." Yvonne nodded. "For now, I have questions regarding other matters. I need to put those to Rob as a matter of urgency."

"I'll fetch the DNA results." Mason rose from his seat.

"DI Mason is leaving the room." Yvonne turned her gaze back to Payne. "Who are you blackmailing at the moment, Rob?"

"Blackmail? I thought I was being charged with murder?" Rob tapped his fingers on the desk. "A murder I didn't commit," he mumbled.

"I know you've been blackmailing pilots." She was bending the truth, again, but felt justified under the circumstances.

Rob stared at her.

She could see him analysing, trying to work out if she was bluffing. She sat back, arms folded controlling her breathing. "Give me a name," she pushed. "Tell me who you've got dangling on a leash."

"If you knew I was blackmailing someone, you'd have the name. You're fishing. Is arresting me for a murder I didn't commit not enough for you? Now you have to get me on a blackmail charge as well? Your life dull, is it? Policing boring round here, is it? I should think all these air disasters give you a bit of excitement, don't they?" He leered at her.

"Does it excite you? Is that why you do it?"

He gritted his teeth; the colour rising in his cheeks. The barely controlled violence of his temper was palpable.

"Your life dull, is it? College going badly? Jealous of pilots who have passed their test? All the above?"

"You don't know what you are talking about." He clicked his tongue at her, jerking his head back.

"So, enlighten me. Give me names. Give me a better idea."

"No comment."

"We have enough to hold you for days, Rob. And, we will. Better to give the information sooner rather than later."

Rob made a point of looking at his watch, flicking his gaze between it and Yvonne's face.

"Well?"

"You're too late." The arrogance was back.

Her stomach knotted. A wave of nausea coursed through her. "What do you mean, too late? What have you done?"

"No comment."

"Rob? What's happening?"

"No comment."

DI Mason returned with copies of the DNA results to give to Payne's solicitor.

Yvonne pushed her chair back. "Interview suspended."

∽

"What's happening?" Mason followed her out of the room.

"We'll let him consult with his solicitor. Do me a favour, would you?"

"Sure."

"Take Dewi and go in with Simon Jones. Ask him for the name of the pilot being blackmailed by Payne. Tell him, we know that's what's happening."

"Do you have anything to twist his arm with?"

"Only further charges of conspiracy to blackmail, if he doesn't come clean."

"Okay."

"Phil, it's urgent. I think a pilot is about to crash. Do everything you can to get a name. Call me immediately, if you get one."

"Right."

MELISSA'S STARE was less belligerent, as Yvonne crossed the floor to retake her seat opposite. Instead, her eyes flickered between those of the DI's, in an attempt to read her.

"Melissa. We have had confirmation that the blood, on the clothing fragments we found in Rob Payne's garden, belonged to Gethin Jenkins. It directly implicates your friend in the murder."

Melissa's eyes dropped to the desk.

"I'm not accusing you of involvement, at this stage, but I need you to be honest with me. I can't help you if you are not."

Melissa bit her lip.

Yvonne's phone vibrated in her pocket. She checked the screen. It was a text from Dai. She turned her face back to the girl. "Payne has admitted to blackmailing a pilot and tells me this pilot is at risk. Now. Today."

The girl's eyes stayed on the table in front.

"I believe you're a member of his gang. The Hand of Darkness."

Melissa's widened eyes moved back to the DI's face. She chewed her lips.

"Your gang has been blackmailing pilots. We know this. What we don't know is the name of the pilot at risk. I need you to give me that name."

Melissa pushed her chair back and stood. "You can't keep me here. You've got nothing on me. I'm going."

"Sit down, Melissa," Yvonne ordered. "I could charge you with conspiracy to pervert the course of justice. Trying to cover up a murder."

"You can't. You don't have any evidence."

"No? Uniform have been speaking to Robert Payne's

neighbours." Yvonne lifted her phone and waved it in front of her. "I've just had it confirmed that they saw you, Matt Jakes, and Simon Jones in Payne's back garden, burning stuff."

Melissa gaped, tugging strands of her hair.

"Who are you blackmailing, Melissa? Who is going up in the air today?"

No answer.

Yvonne leaned across the desk, her voice deceptively soft. "Give me a name."

Melissa whispered with her solicitor.

"Can I have immunity, if I give you a name?"

Yvonne closed her eyes, holding back what she would like to say. "I can't promise you immunity for everything, but it is possible we could drop the conspiracy to pervert the course of justice charge, since you were not responsible for Gethin Jenkins' actual murder. I'd have to run it past my superior, but I could make that case."

"What about the blackmail?"

Yvonne shook her head. "I can't promise you that." The DI made a point of looking at her watch. "However, if you do not give me a name, more pilots will probably die and you will face even more charges."

Melissa looked at her solicitor, who nodded.

"Thomas. Royston Thomas."

"Where is he flying from?"

"I don't know."

"Which airport?"

"I don't know."

"Then, you will face every single charge you deserve to."

"Welshpool. It's Welshpool." Melissa broke down.

Yvonne rushed from her seat.

"Interview suspended."

"Callum, call Welshpool Airport. A Royston Thomas is due to fly from there today. Tell them to halt his flight. He is not to go up under any circumstances."

"Right, ma'am."

"Then I want you to speak to the DCI. Inform him of the DNA results on the clothing found at Payne's address and tell him we have an active situation regarding risk to a pilot. We'll need an alert to go out to all light aircraft pilots in the area, in case Royston Thomas has made it into the air. The DCI can organise that. He has more clout."

"On it."

"Emergency services will need to be on standby."

"On standby, where?"

"I don't know, but likely in the Welshpool area."

"Okay."

"Dewi?"

"Ma'am?"

"We're heading to the airport. Let's go."

29

NEAR MISS

Royston went through his checklist one last time before his buddy cleared him for takeoff.

He knew the route. Knew how dangerous the mission was. These pilots did not mess around. Likely, he wouldn't even see them coming. But they would see him and, with lightening fast reactions and highly sensitive controls, they would avoid him. It was his best chance. His life in their hands. Their lives in their hands. Pray God, they were safe hands.

What he couldn't understand, was why the gang had not been in touch. His dash cam would capture the near miss, but he had expected them to check that he was going up today. Instead, he had received nothing, like they had stopped caring whether he went.

As he started down the runway, he was thankful of the clear sky and lack of wind. That guaranteed suitable flying weather for the target aircraft. He didn't know when they would come through, but if he hung around long enough, he was sure that they would.

~

"Thank God for the bypass," Yvonne muttered, as they sped between roundabouts on the way to the airport.

Her phone rang at full volume.

"Callum?"

"Yes, ma'am. The airport confirmed that Thomas's plane is already in the air."

"What?"

"They are attempting to contact him, to ask him to return."

"What do you mean attempting? Are they having trouble getting hold of him?"

"He hadn't responded, when I spoke to them a moment ago."

"We've got to get him down. Okay, Callum, we're nearly at the airport. I'll let them know how urgent the situation is. Thanks. Keep me informed of what's happening your end."

~

They parked at speed, dumping their vehicle at an angle. Yvonne ran to the offices, followed by Dewi. The latter ran to close the car door she left open in her haste.

She found the air-to-ground staff supporting each other in the office. They were two females, one of whom was on the radio, and the other stood, hands on hips next to her, face contorted with angst.

"DI Giles." Yvonne flashed her warrant card. "Is she talking to Royston Thomas?" she asked of the female not on the radio.

The woman ran both hands through her shoulder-length, fair hair. "He's not answering. We don't know why. Has something happened?"

"God, I hope not." Yvonne ran forward "Do we know where he is?"

The woman checked the nearest computer screen. "We've called in the help of NATS. They have the radar tech that lets us know where aircraft are, when we have an emergency like this. According to them, he's still in the air and heading south-west towards Machynlleth."

"Machynlleth?" Yvonne frowned. "Please keep trying to get hold of him."

"Yvonne," Dewi grabbed her arm. "The Mach loop. The American military fly the Mach loop, Monday to Friday. It is the area between Machynlleth and Dolgellau. They do all the low-flying exercises there. They go down as low as one hundred feet."

"Oh God, is he looking to do a near miss with an American jet? That would be suicide, surely?"

"He's still not answering." The woman on the radio shrugged her shoulders at the DI. "What do you want us to do?"

"Dewi, contact the station and ask them to make the military aware of the situation. They can send up a plane to intercept him, if we haven't persuaded him to turn around." Yvonne turned back to the women in the office. "Could you speak to him as though he is listening? Let him know the police know what the blackmailers asked him to do and tell him he is to abort the mission. He does not have to go through with it. We've got the gang in custody. He'll know what you mean."

As the dark-haired female called through the radio, the other checked the screen again, before turning back to Yvonne. "What are we dealing with? Is he a terrorist?"

Yvonne shook her head. "No, but we believe he is being blackmailed into committing a dangerous act. I can't say much more than that at the moment, and I do not have all the details, yet, but I can say that both Royston Thomas's plane, and possibly a military jet, are at risk unless we can get Thomas to abort the mission he thinks he has to complete."

Sirens going off outside told of the emergency services arrival.

Dewi finished his call to Callum and came to her side.

Yvonne's phone rang. It was the DCI.

"Yvonne, what's happening? Have they got hold of the pilot?"

She brought Llewelyn up to speed. "Sir, I've asked the radio operators to ask Thomas to turn around, in case he's listening. I've asked them to explain that we have the gang in custody."

She could hear the tremor in his voice. It matched her own. He was as scared as she was. "Has he responded?"

"Not yet, sir. They will keep trying. In the meantime, they are having help from a radar unit, keeping tabs on him. He's still heading towards Machynlleth, as far as we know."

"Wait a minute, I've got another call." Llewelyn put her on hold.

Yvonne raised her eyebrows in inquiry, towards the woman on the radio who shook her head in response. The DI ran a hand through her hair, her heart thumping in her chest.

The DCI came back on. "Right, the Americans at the base are now aware. Their jet is already in the air, but they have informed the pilots there could be a rogue aircraft around and they are keeping their eyes open."

Yvonne allowed herself a deep breath. "Well, that's

something. We've still had no response from his plane." The DI put her hand over the phone, as she spoke to the girl on the radio. "Please run through the instructions to Royston Thomas again. He's got to be listening."

The woman nodded.

"Sorry, sir, we are doing everything we can. We've got fire engines and ambulances on standby at the airport, in case he comes back this way and anything happens here. I just wish he would respond."

The woman watching the screens interrupted them. "He's turned around. According to NATS, he has turned North, and is heading back this way."

Yvonne sighed. "Let's hope that's a good sign. Why isn't he responding?"

At that moment, a broken transmission came through on the radio.

"I think that's him." The radio operator shouted, before requesting that the caller repeat his last.

"I've got to go, sir. I think we've gotten through to the pilot."

She heard him sigh with relief. "Right. Keep me informed."

Yvonne rang off and ran to the radio operator who was speaking to Royston. "You'll be clear to land. Take it steady."

"How long until he is back?" Yvonne put a hand to her chest, taking a deep breath to slow her thudding heart.

"We think about fifteen minutes."

"Thank you." Yvonne rubbed the woman's arm. "Well done, getting hold of him."

30

TOUCHDOWN

Royston's Piper touched down, as an ambulance and fire engine moved towards the runway.

Thankfully, Royston didn't need them.

Yvonne breathed. It was a perfect landing, both wheels touching tarmac at the same time. A minor miracle, given what the pilot had been through.

She waited outside of the main hangar for the plane to come to a halt. As her legs shook, she placed a hand on the wall to steady herself, all the while continuing to take deep breaths.

∽

"You will arrest me, won't you?" Royston Thomas had deep lines under his hollowed, bloodshot eyes. The sagging skin told the story of the umpteen sleepless nights the pilot had been through.

Dewi had hold of his arm as they led him through to the office, intending on giving him a coffee before taking him to the station.

The DI pursed her lips. "You were going to fly your aircraft at an American military jet, in what would have been a reckless life-threatening act. It wasn't just your life at risk, but God knows how many others."

He hung his head. "They had me over a barrel."

"You put yourself over the barrel. They merely led you to it. Why the hell didn't you come to us?" Yvonne sighed. "That's what we are here for. To serve the public without fear or favour. We could have sorted this out a long time ago." She thought of Gethin Jenkins, perhaps he would still be alive.

"I would have lost my wife. They told me the girl was underage. They threatened to go to police, saying I'd been having sex with her. I didn't even meet with her, let alone do anything. We only talked. I thought no-one would believe me. I thought Karen would leave me. She still might."

"Then, it is up to you to sort it with her. Talk to her, man. Be honest with her. Give her the chance to make up her own mind, and let her do so while you are being authentic, and not the ideal person you think she needs you to be. If there's something missing from your marriage, promise each other you'll work on it. Together. Keep talking to each other."

Royston nodded.

Yvonne gestured towards uniformed officers standing by. "Take him in."

31

DEBRIEF

"Melissa Hines was the honey pot." Dewi shook his head as he poured water on their teabags, at the table that served as their coffee area, at the back of CID.

"Yes. They had quite a little scheme going." Yvonne stirred the mugs for him. "They sourced their pilots well, choosing the ones known to have suffered depression or were otherwise vulnerable. Rob could get that information from his dad, and from snippets of conversation he was hearing in the hangars. I wondered why he was always hanging around. For an aviation enthusiast, he looked remarkably sullen and uninterested, whenever I saw him."

"And Melissa would contact the pilots on social media."

"Yes. She contacted them out of the blue and formed friendships with them. The chat always turned to the possibility of meeting up, and always with the suggestion there could be more to the friendship. She would then either delete the conversations from her end, or remind the men to delete them in case their wives found out. She used fake profiles as extra insurance. The gang gradually took over and controlled the minds of those men."

"Frightening stuff."

"You can say that again."

"Frightening stuff."

"Oh, you are hilarious." Yvonne sipped her tea. "Dewi, there's something I've been meaning to tell you. I want you to keep it to yourself, for now. I'll speak to the others when I can."

"Ooh, sounds mysterious. What are you up to?" Dewi grinned.

"It's about Tasha." Yvonne took a deep breath. "She's moved in with me."

"Makes sense." Dewi nodded. "Seems daft, her always having to travel back and forth whenever she gives us a hand."

"No, I mean she's moved in with me. We're living together." Yvonne frowned.

"Oh. Oh, you mean *moved in*."

"Yes, now you get it." Yvonne cast a look around behind her. "We're together. We love each other. Close your mouth, Dewi. Is there a problem because she's a woman?"

"No. No, of course not. I'm just gob smacked you've finally made a commitment to someone. With anyone. Well done, you. I'm happy for you. I'm sure when you get around to telling the rest of the team, they'll be happy for you too."

"I thought, for a moment there..."

Dewi gave her full on hug. "Bloody well done, ma'am. It's about time. Here's to you and your misses." He raised his mug to clink with hers. "Good on you."

Yvonne smiled with relief, raising her mug. "Cheers. Thank you, Dewi."

"I HEAR CONGRATULATIONS ARE IN ORDER." Tasha gave a broad smile, as she tossed down the copy of the County Times she found on the train from Shrewsbury. "That's a great photo of you."

Yvonne examined the picture, taken on the runway at Welshpool Airport, and grimaced. "Oh dear, I hate it when they put me on the front cover."

"Get on with you." Tasha gave her a nudge. "You love it, really."

Yvonne hugged her hard, taking the psychologist's bag, and putting it down next to the fire. "It's been a nightmare of a week. It's been a nightmare month. And I am so thrilled to see you."

"Looks like it ended well enough." Tasha hugged her back. "And I expected no less from the most brilliant detective in these parts."

Yvonne poked the fire and threw on another couple of logs. "How's the London Met case coming along?"

"We're done. We set up a successful sting and stopped a vicious rapist in his tracks. His targets were all high profile people who would rather their names stayed out of the papers than put a dangerous predator away. He's been at it for years, mostly because of their reluctance to come forward."

"Were they afraid for their reputations?"

"Until he picked the wrong one, yes. He knew what he was doing. He made the mistake of underestimating one of his victims. Thank god for her bravery."

"Well then, it looks like we have a double reason to celebrate." Yvonne pressed a kiss to Tasha's cheek. "I'll go get the glasses."

"What's that gorgeous smell coming from in there?" Tasha lifted her nose in the air, following Yvonne into the kitchen.

"Homemade, lamb Madras curry. Be warned, it's hot. I needed to use up the chillies. I'm making saffron rice to go with it."

Tasha giggled. "Good job I like hot. Better give me a large glass of that wine, though, just in case."

∽

As they seated themselves to eat, Yvonne reached her hand across the table to clasp Tasha's, her eyes shining. "I've something to tell you. I think you'll approve."

Tasha tilted her head. "What is it, Inspector Giles? I'm intrigued."

"Do you remember the conversation we had, the day you left to begin the case with the Met?"

"Remind me?"

"We were talking about the possibility of you having further work with our team."

"Have you got something for me?"

"At the moment, we haven't. That wasn't the entire conversation, though. You wanted to know if I had told anyone about us being a couple. Do you remember that?"

"Ah, yes, I do." Tasha nodded.

"You seemed disappointed when I told you I hadn't mentioned it to any of my colleagues and, I have to admit, I felt guilty about that. I felt like I'd let you down and I never want to let you down."

Tasha squeezed her hand. "You silly thing, you needn't have worried. I'm a big girl, and I know these things take time. The moment has to be right for you. Coming out to friends and family is never easy. I respect your need to do it in your own time. You know your friends better than I do. Any disappointment I had, was fleeting, and was more with myself, and my own expectations, than with you."

"I told Dewi." Yvonne's smile lit her face. "I told him yesterday, over a cuppa."

Tasha mused that the DI looked years younger. The disclosure had taken a load off her. "You did?"

"I did. I haven't told the others yet, but I will, one-by-one."

Tasha rose from the table to give her a hug. "How did he take it? I'm so proud of you."

"He was fine. He told me he'd almost given up on my making a commitment to anyone."

Tasha laughed. "I bagged the elusive DI Giles. Aren't I just the luckiest woman alive?"

"Oh, give over." Yvonne giggled despite herself. "I was waiting for the right one to come along. Only, the right one was patiently waiting in the wings for me, all along. Thank you for waiting, Tasha. I don't believe I deserved it, but I'm glad you did."

"You are worth waiting for. I don't think you realise how much we all love you, or how much you deserve love."

"Likewise." Yvonne began clearing the plates. "Now, about working with the team. I'll speak to the DCI next week and see if we can get you on a more permanent footing. The powers that be are investing in Welsh crime fighting at the moment. We should strike while the iron is hot."

"Sounds hopeful." Tasha smiled. "Now, let's eat this gorgeous curry."

The End

AFTERWORD

Mailing list: You can join my emailing list here : AnnamarieMorgan.com

Facebook page: AnnamarieMorganAuthor

You might also like to read the other books in the series:
   Book 1: Death Master:
   After months of mental and physical therapy, Yvonne Giles, an Oxford DI, is back at work and that's just how she likes it. So when she's asked to hunt the serial killer responsible for taking apart young women, the DI jumps at the chance but hides the fact she is suffering debilitating flashbacks. She is told to work with Tasha Phillips, an in-her-face, criminal psychologist. The DI is not enamoured with the idea. Tasha has a lot to prove. Yvonne has a lot to get over. A tentative link with a 20 year-old cold case brings them closer to the truth but events then take a horrifyingly personal turn.

Book 2: You Will Die

After apprehending an Oxford Serial Killer, and almost losing her life in the process, DI Yvonne Giles has left England for a quieter life in rural Wales. Her peace is shattered when she is asked to hunt a priest-killing psychopath, who taunts the police with messages inscribed on the corpses. Yvonne requests the help of Dr. Tasha Phillips, a psychologist and friend, to aid in the hunt. But the killer is one step ahead and the ultimatum, he sets them, could leave everyone devastated.

Book 3: Total Wipeout

A whole family is wiped out with a shotgun. At first glance, it's an open-and-shut case. The dad did it, then killed himself. The deaths follow at least two similar family wipeouts – attributed to the financial crash.

So why doesn't that sit right with Detective Inspector Yvonne Giles? And why has a rape occurred in the area, in the weeks preceding each family's demise? Her seniors do not believe there are questions to answer. DI Giles must therefore risk everything, in a high-stakes investigation of a mysterious masonic ring and players in high finance.

Can she find the answers, before the next innocent family is wiped out?

Book 4: Deep Cut

In a tiny hamlet in North Wales, a female recruit is murdered whilst on Christmas home leave. Detective Inspector Yvonne Giles is asked to cut short her own leave, to investigate. Why was the young soldier killed? And is her death related to several alleged suicides at her army base? DI Giles this it is, and that someone powerful has a dark secret they will do anything to hide.

Book 5: The Pusher

Young men are turning up dead on the banks of the River Severn. Some of them have been missing for days or even weeks. The only thing the police can be sure of, is that the men have drowned. Rumours abound that a mythical serial killer has turned his attention from the Manchester canal to the waterways of Mid-Wales. And now one of CID's own is missing. A brand new recruit with everything to live for. DI Giles must find him before it's too late.

Book 6: Gone

Children are going missing. They are not heard from again until sinister requests for cryptocurrency go viral. The public must pay or the children die. For lead detective Yvonne Giles, the case is complicated enough. And then the unthinkable happens...

Book 7: Bone Dancer

A serial killer is murdering women, threading their bones back together, and leaving them for police to find. Detective Inspector Yvonne Giles must find him before more innocent victims die. Problem is, the killer wants her and will do anything he can to get her. Unaware that she, herself, is is a target, DI Giles risks everything to catch him.

Book 8: Blood Lost

A young man comes home to find his whole family missing. Half-eaten breakfasts and blood spatter on the lounge wall are the only clues to what happened...

Book 9: Angel of Death

He is watching. Biding his time. Preparing himself for a

torturous kill. Soaring above; lord of all. His journey, direct through the lives of the unsuspecting.

The Angel of Death is nigh.

The peace of the Mid-Wales countryside is shattered, when a female eco-warrior is found crucified in a public wood. At first, it would appear a simple case of finding which of the woman's enemies had had her killed. But DI Yvonne Giles has no idea how bad things are going to get. As the body count rises, she will need all of her instincts, and the skills of those closest to her, to stop the murderous rampage of the Angel of Death.

Printed in Poland
by Amazon Fulfillment
Poland Sp. z o.o., Wrocław